Praise for *Heart Craving*

"This little sizzler will leave you breathless."
—*Bell, Book & Candle*

"Sandra Hill delivers a spicy, sexy romp about a man desperate enough to try anything to salvage his marriage."
—*Jill Smith,* Romantic Times Magazine

"Sunflowers, tattoos, mega-sized cats, and VW convertibles make this a story to remember . . . Burning passions that scorch the pages . . . Sandra's pen is really smoking."
—*Karen Ellington,* The Literary Times

". . . few authors can fuse erotica with drop-dead humor like Hill."
—*Publishers Weekly*

Other Sandra Hill Titles from Bell Bridge Books

Saving Savannah
(a novella)

A Dixie Christmas
(anthology)

Santa Viking
(anthology)

'Twas the Night
(with Trish Jensen and Kate Holmes)

Heart Craving

by

Sandra Hill

Bell Bridge Books

This is a work of fiction. Names, characters, places and incidents are either the products of the author's imagination or are used fictitiously. Any resemblance to actual persons (living or dead), events or locations is entirely coincidental.

Bell Bridge Books
PO BOX 300921
Memphis, TN 38130
Print ISBN: 978-1-61194-510-2

Bell Bridge Books is an Imprint of BelleBooks, Inc.

Printed and bound in the United States of America.

A mass market edition of this book was published in the LOVESCAPE anthology from Leisure Books in 1996

We at BelleBooks enjoy hearing from readers.
Visit our websites
BelleBooks.com
BellBridgeBooks.com.
ImaJinnBooks.com

10 9 8 7 6 5 4 3 2 1

Cover design: Debra Dixon
Interior design: Hank Smith
Photo/Art credits:
Couple (manipulated) © Mystock88photo | Dreamstime.com

:Lchy:01:

Dedication

To all women, regardless of age or culture or background, who yearn for those ethereal things men do not understand: "heart cravings."

To those good men who try, but just don't get it.

And especially to those men who try and do get it. Their women are the luckiest of all.

Chapter One

You can't keep a good man down . . . uh, out . . .

NICK DICELLO POUNDED on the apartment door with one fist. The other clutched the legal document he'd just received from the subpoena server he'd been dodging for weeks.

"Paula! Paula, are you in there? Answer the door!"

The only response was the wild barking of a dog.

He took a key out of his back pocket and tried, unsuccessfully, to open the door. "Damn! She must have changed the lock."

Nick pressed his forehead wearily against the cold wood of the doorframe, then stiffened with determination. Paula wasn't going to hide from him this time.

A locked door. No problem. Not for a cop in Newark, New Jersey. Hell! Not for a guy who'd grown up on the streets of Newark, either.

Pulling a flat leather pouch from the inside pocket of his sport coat, he selected a small tool. Within seconds, he was inside.

He braced himself for the sound of her security alarm, but silence greeted him. *The same old Paula!* he thought, with disgust. He closed the door after him and checked the keypad. Yep, despite his nagging, she'd forgotten once again to turn on the alarm system.

The dog leaped forward then and almost knocked him to the floor. Backing him up against the wall, the huge German shepherd stood on its hind legs and put its lethal front paws on his chest.

"How ya doin', Gonzo?"

The dog lapped his tongue across Nick's face in reply.

He pushed the dog aside with an affectionate ruffle of his fur and walked around the familiar room, checking the door with its numerous locks, the windows, and the high tech, direct-link police security console—unplugged and obviously never used.

Satisfied that everything was okay, Nick dropped down into a chair, planning to wait for Paula's return. He flicked on the remote for the TV and surfed the channels, stopping at *A Woman's Edge, with Dr. Sheila Storm.*

Lord, what do women see in this broad?

Dr. Sheila was interviewing a bunch of psycho psychics who claimed they could help people improve their love lives.

"Hah!" he remarked to Gonzo, who sprawled at his feet adoringly. It was nice to have someone show a little appreciation for him. Even if it was only a dog.

Pointing to the TV, he told Gonzo, "Women believe all this relationship crap, you know, but we men know better."

"Woof!" Gonzo agreed.

"If women would just tell men what they really want, instead of expecting us dumb schmucks to figure it out on our own, there wouldn't be any need for scam shrinks. Or divorce," he added bleakly.

Gonzo gave him one of those male looks that said, "Women! Go figure!"

"So, how's your love life, boy? Better than mine, I hope."

Before Gonzo had a chance to respond, Nick heard water running in the bathroom down the hall. The shower. *Uh-oh!* Paula was home, after all.

Briefly, he considered joining her for a quick one.

Nah, she's gonna be mad enough that I've broken into the apartment.

On the other hand . . .

He couldn't stop picturing Paula. He knew exactly how she'd look. Her shoulder-length auburn hair slicked back wetly. Soap bubbles covering the nipples of her full breasts, sliding down her flat belly, through silky curls, onto her long, long legs.

Oh, hell!

His heart slammed against his chest wall, and he swallowed

hard, forcing himself to look back at the TV, where another loony bird was now advising that men should find out what women crave.

Nick tried to listen, but he was unable to stop thinking about Paula in the shower. Remembering. And a long-neglected part of his body—the one with no common sense at all—jump-started into a full-blown, mind-blistering hard-on.

It had been *way* too long.

He slipped off his loafers, then his socks. Just testing, he told himself. He wasn't *really* stupid enough to try joining her in the shower. Mentally patting himself on the back for his great self-control, he decided, like brain-dead men throughout the ages, to test himself just a little bit more by removing his slacks and jacket and shirt.

And the intelligence cells in his brain melted.

Testosterone took charge.

"Maybe Paula wouldn't really mind my company. Maybe she's as horny as I am."

Gonzo rolled his eyes. That was doggie for, "It's your funeral, buddy."

Rub-a-dub-dub, clueless man style . . .

PAULA STOOD UNDER the shower, her face raised to the warm spray. She'd been there a long time, but still the tears kept coming.

Her lawyer had called a little while ago to tell her that the divorce papers had finally been served on Nick. Their hearing would be in one week.

"So, it's finally over," she said aloud.

"Never!" a harsh voice said, and Paula jumped with shock.

Nick opened the shower doors and stepped inside, totally, gloriously nude. At first, relief flooded over her that it wasn't a stranger who'd broken into her apartment. But her relief soon turned to outrage.

"Nick, get out! You know our lawyers said we shouldn't be talking."

"Actually, it wasn't talking I had in mind." He smiled at her crookedly, his black hair already wet, beads of water rolling down his neck onto his broad shoulders.

Paula recognized the gleam of passion in his pale blue eyes, and it was impossible to ignore the powerful arousal standing out from his body—what Nick used to call a "blue steeler," a particularly virile erection.

"No, Nick. My lawyer says we should stay away from each other. Let alone . . . you know." She backed up against the tile wall and Nick followed. A predator, dangerous and out of control.

"What do lawyers know?" he murmured, pressing his body up against her, rubbing his crisp chest hairs against her sensitive skin. He moaned huskily with appreciation. "You're my wife. I'm your husb—"

"No! We haven't been husband and wife for a year," she cried out and pushed against his chest, to no avail. "You creep! The last time I saw you was at Casey's Tavern a month ago. You were three sheets to the wind, and your arm was wrapped around Sheila Zeppenzipper."

"Zapper," he corrected, putting his hands on her waist and nuzzling her neck.

"Huh?" Paula's mind was fast turning fuzzy as Nick's hands cupped her bottom and lifted her, parting her legs in the process. He fitted her to his hardness and moved against her rhythmically.

"Zeppenzapper, not zipper." He lifted her higher so her breasts came level with his mouth, her toes barely touching the floor.

"Aaarrgh!" Paula wasn't sure if she groaned over his semantics, or the excruciating pleasure of his mouth suckling her.

"And the reason I was drinking"—he explained with deceptive calmness, deliberately teasing her by pulling away, aware that she didn't want him to stop—"is that I saw you on the other side of the room with your friends. And you were ignoring me. And I wanted to make you jealous."

"Jealous! You're a fool."

"I know." He appeared contrite with his black hair plastered to his head and water dripping down the fine bones of his face, like a little boy, but his innocent look was belied by the expert fingers working their magic between their bodies.

"You were trying to make me . . . oh, my . . . ah . . . jealous?" Her knees grew weak, and she tilted her hips forward, reflexively, accommodating his intimate caresses. "After punching Jerry Sullivan . . . stop that"—she slapped his hand away, only to have it move to another equally erotic place—"in the nose . . . the week before? Just because he delivered some . . . some . . . legal papers to my . . . uh . . . apartment?" She knew she was blabbering incoherently. She couldn't help herself.

Paula hated her weakness. After refusing to see or talk to Nick in person the past year, how could she suddenly succumb to his advances? It must be because he'd caught her off guard, she told herself. And because, with the delivery of the divorce papers today, the clock had begun counting down the final hours of their marriage. Only seven more days.

"There's a perfectly good explanation." He brushed her lips with his, back and forth, coaxing her to open for him.

She jerked her head aside. "Huh? What explanation?"

He chucked her under the chin, knowing the effect he was having on her, and loving it. "An explanation as to why I punched Jerry Sullivan, honey. I thought he was your date."

"Oh, you are incredible! He's my lawyer, for God's sake! But even if he was my date, you had no right to hit him."

"I know. I know." He closed his eyes on a deep moan as he lifted her once again, wrapping her legs around his waist.

She could barely hear over the roar of blood in her ears.

Taking his erection in his own hand, he placed himself against her.

"What did you say?" she choked out.

"I . . . don't . . . know," he whispered on a gasp. Before he'd barely entered her body, she began to convulse around him. "That . . . feels . . . so-o-o . . . good."

It was her turn to gasp.

Trembling with hard-fought restraint, Nick embedded himself in her with one long stroke and began to push her against the shower wall. The stall shook with the force of his thrusts.

Her orgasm never stopped.

Over and over he moved inside her, hard, violent plunges into her woman's center.

The small spirals of her climax widened, becoming harsher, longer in duration.

Nick seemed to grow larger inside her body's sheath, reaching for her very womb.

It was over in minutes.

His neck arched backward with a guttural growl of masculine release.

Paula felt him jerk inside her, and she shuddered once more with a violent internal convulsion.

Drawing in deep draughts of air, Nick finally pulled away and let her feet slide to the floor. The shower continued to pelt them both with its hot spray.

Leaning back against the opposite wall, fighting for breath, he said, "I love you, Paula."

Then he grinned with typical male self-satisfaction.

He probably expected her to swoon and say, "Oh, Nick, you are so wonderful. I forgive you everything."

Instead, she swung her arm in a wide arc and punched him in the stomach.

Love hurts, for sure . . .

FIFTEEN MINUTES later, Paula padded into the living room in her bare feet, having donned only jeans and a T-shirt. She was still drying her hair with a towel.

"Nick, I told you to leave," she said testily.

He'd combed his thick black hair off his face, but it was still wet from their shower. She tried to shut off her sensual awareness of him, but memories assaulted her. How many times, over how many years, had she seen him looking just like this?

She had trouble swallowing over the lump in her throat.

He was sitting in front of the television, fully dressed in khaki, pleated slacks, open-collared Oxford shirt, and navy blazer, watching *The Woman's Edge*.

Dr. Sheila? Nick?

His long fingers were idly stroking Gonzo's fur. The traitorous beast sat at his feet, making doggie sounds of slavish ecstasy. A lot like she had a short time ago.

Oh, Lord!

"We have to talk, Paula." He waved the divorce papers at her angrily.

"Like we just did in the shower?"

"I didn't plan that. That's not why I came over here."

"Hah! The devil made you do it, then?" She threw down her towel with disgust and finger-combed her hair back off her face.

"Nah, it was some other . . . being," he countered and winked, looking down between his legs.

Well, she'd stepped into that one. But she'd had enough of his foolishness.

"Listen here, you big jerk. Don't ever, *ever*, break into my apartment again and assault me. Because, believe me, I'll have you arrested. And don't think I can't."

"Assault! Hey, you're suffering a memory lapse here, babe." His strong chin lifted with affront. "You wanted it as much as I did."

She felt her face flame. "Yeah, well, it's not going to happen ever again. I'll get a restraining order if I have to. I mean it. This marriage is over." *So, why do I feel like he'll always be mine?*

"If you think a restraining order would stop me, you've got another thing—"

Holding up a hand to halt his bitter words, Paula tried another tack. "While you're here, Nick, there is something I wanted to tell you." Her voice softened. "I got my master's degree last week. Finally."

"Oh, Paula, that's wonderful!"

She knew that Nick's enthusiasm was genuine. She'd been an elementary school teacher, attending college at night the past three years to get a master's degree in social work. He, more than anyone, knew how much time and heart she'd put into her studies.

He stood and opened his arms for her, to hug her in congratulation. She ducked and stepped away. No way could she risk the temptation of his touch. Again.

Suddenly, he seemed to think of something, and an emotion like fear transformed his handsome face. "You're not . . . oh, no . . . don't tell me. You're not quitting your job, are you?"

"Yes, I am. I have a couple of interviews set up, including the Patterson Projects, as a youth activity coordinator."

"No! That's a DMZ, the most dangerous section of the city. You can't!"

"Yes, I can, Nick, and there's nothing you can do about it. And while we're on the subject, I want you to stop having patrols go by here every night. I'm a grown woman, not a baby. I can take care of myself."

Nick cringed as all the old arguments resonated between them. This was not the point of her telling him her news.

"Paula, honey, let's not fight."

"Don't you *honey* me. And fighting is the only thing we do well anymore."

"Not everything," he reminded her gently.

"O-o-oh! It's just like you to think a quick romp in the shower is the answer to everything. Wham-bam, and I'm the cream in your coffee again. You are so predictable."

He flinched at her uncharacteristic crudeness. Nick hated it when she used street talk. He always wanted her to be up on this impossible nice-girls-don't pedestal.

"Give me another chance. We can work things out."

"Nick, don't do this," she cried. "You and I have talked till we're blue in the face. It's over. Dammit, it's over." Her voice cracked with the last words.

Nick's face flushed with angry resolve. He wasn't a man who accepted defeat easily. "Over? Never! I've made mistakes, but—"

"Nick, stop it. Stop it right now."

"Paula, I love you . . ."

She started to cry.

". . . and I think you love me, too . . ."

She hiccupped.

". . . let me just hold you, sweetheart . . ."

She blew her nose.

". . . and maybe we can discover what your . . . ah, problem is . . . what you really want."

She could tell by the stunned look on his face that he immediately regretted his poor choice of words.

"My problem?" she shrieked, her mood changing like quicksilver. "You think I have a problem?"

"That's not what I meant, honey."

"Let me tell you something, Nick—you're right. I do have a problem. I crave things you will apparently never understand. And that's what this divorce is all about. How can a guy who's so smart be so dumb? I'll see you in court in one week, you turkey. Be there!"

Seconds later, standing out in the hall with the door shut behind him, Nick shook his head. He felt like he'd been blindsided with a sucker punch.

Women!

He didn't need a crystal ball or a psycho psychic, like the one jabbering away on *The Woman's Edge*, to realize he'd screwed up again. But he didn't exactly understand where he'd gone wrong, either.

One week. Seven lousy days.

Maybe he needed some outside help.

Chapter Two

Day One
All he needed was a little advice. Or a lot . . .

"CRAZY . . . out-of-this-world crazy . . . that's what I must be."

Nick continued to mutter as he stepped gingerly up the rickety staircase of the faded yellow structure, wondering whether the rotting planks would hold his 210 pounds. Hell, it would serve him right if he fell and cracked his thick skull. It would be just payment for the stupidest damn thing he'd ever considered doing in all his thirty-five years.

Nick looked furtively back over his shoulder at the busy highway, hoping no one would recognize him entering such an establishment. He'd never live it down. Never.

Grimacing with self-disgust, Nick knocked on the door before he lost his nerve. Tapping his foot impatiently, he studied the hand-lettered sign in the grimy window: MADAME NADINE: FORTUNE TELLING, LOVE POTIONS, MIRACLES. And in smaller letters at the bottom: HAIR WAXING AND TATTOOS, BY APPOINTMENT.

He should turn around and go home.

But the prospect of another night alone turned his blood cold. Besides, he had only seven days left until . . . until . . . oh, God!

Nick took a deep, painful breath. He felt like a vise was squeezing his heart.

This time he rapped harder, and the door was jerked open.

"C'mon in, honey. I been expectin' you."

Nick's mouth dropped open incredulously, but not at the words of invitation.

The woman standing before him—only a few inches shorter than his six-foot-one—had stuffed her big-boned, overweight body into a tight purple dress covered with huge yellow sunflowers. Lots of sunflowers. So bright they made his eyes water.

A cigarette hung from her crimson lips, its long ash threatening to fall onto her mammoth bosom at any moment. Its acrid odor filled the air, and smoke streamed about in misty, eerie clouds.

"Whattaya mean, you've been expecting me?" Nick finally choked out.

"You been drivin' by every day for weeks, too proud to ask for my help." She flashed him a toothy, gloating smile. "Guess you weren't desperate enough . . . till today."

Yup, desperate, that's me. Desperate and nuts.

Nick followed the floozy into a bright sitting room with windows on three sides and dozens of pots filled with flowers of every variety imaginable. Outside, the heads of sunflowers the size of hubcaps peeped over the windowsills. He raised an eyebrow in question, and Madame Nadine—he presumed she was Nadine—raised all six of her chins defensively. "We don't got flowers where I come from."

Where's that? he wondered. *Probably prison.*

"Are you a Gypsy?" he asked suddenly. Weren't Gypsies supposed to be especially good at fortune-telling and stuff? If she was a Gypsy, maybe she really did have some talent that could help him.

The blowzy babe flashed him a look of utter disbelief. "The only Gypsies I know are moths. You want a Gypsy psychic, you better call one of them 900 numbers."

Nick barely heard her. His eyes kept coming back to the growing ash on her cigarette, amazed that it still held on.

Noticing the direction of his gaze, the fortune-teller added, "We don't got cigarettes where I come from, either." She put her hands on her hips belligerently. "Any objections?"

"Nah, I used to smoke myself."

"I know."

"Huh?"

"Sit down," she ordered, shoving him rudely into a straight-backed chair drawn up to a round table in the center of the room. Immediately, three cats slithered up and rubbed themselves sinuously against his pant leg. He shivered. Lord, he'd hated cats ever since he was a kid in the projects, and the super's answer to rat control was cats. Every time he saw a cat, he remembered . . . well, he remembered too much.

He raised his eyes mutinously to the woman who was easing her ample rear into the chair opposite him. Two more cats ambled in and jumped up onto her wide lap.

"Let me guess. You don't have cats where you come from, either." When she didn't answer, he asked, "Do you charge extra for cat hair?" *Damn, I'll be covered with hair when I get home. Probably smell like cat, too.*

"You've got a smart mouth on you, boy. Be careful, or I won't help you."

His eyes widened hopefully. *Oh, please, God, I need help so bad.* "Can you help me?"

"Do angels have wings?"

"I don't know. Do they?"

Ignoring his sarcasm, Madame Nadine reached under the fringed tablecloth and pulled out a round glass ball, open on one side. She dusted it off on the hem of her dress and plunked it ceremoniously in the center of the table. It was the most pitiful-looking crystal ball he'd ever seen—more like an upended fish bowl, or a ceiling light globe.

"So, what's your problem, sonny? Want a tattoo? Or a body waxing? Yeah, I bet that's it. You're one of them modern manscaped fellas? You want your chest hairs removed so you can be smooth as a baby's butt all over?"

He slapped a hand to his chest defensively. "You're not pluckin' anything from my body. No way!"

"Fortune told?"

"Well . . . maybe." Nick could feel his face flame. But he never blushed. And he'd never been shy about expressing himself before, about *anything.* What was wrong with him? "I was thinking more on the lines of . . . well . . . oh, hell . . . a love potion."

Madame Nadine's ash finally fell into the cleavage of her dress, and she immediately lit up another cigarette. He watched, fascinated, as she blew a waft of smoke his way, which hovered in the air, then swirled about the glass globe, finally filling it with a murky sheen. Then she turned her attention back to him, studying his face with disconcerting thoroughness.

"A love potion ain't gonna do you diddly-squat, sweet cakes. You need *big* help."

Tell me about it! "How do you know?"

Madame Nadine shrugged. "You are one screwed-up hombre. But maybe you're not hopeless yet. Start from the beginning, and let's see if we can unravel this mess you've made of your life."

This was ridiculous. He'd been a fool even to enter this rattrap. The chick was a scam artist if he'd ever seen one, and he ought to know. He stood abruptly and threw a few bills on the table. "Thanks for your trouble, but I've changed my mind."

He hightailed it for the door.

She called after him, "Don't wait too long, sweetie. You only got seven days left."

The fine hairs stood out on his neck as he pivoted slowly. "What did you say?"

"You only got seven days till your divorce is final, hon." She was leaning back in her chair, blowing smoke rings with studied casualness. "If you want to save your marriage, you better not dawdle."

"Who . . . are . . . you?" he asked, spacing his words evenly, as he plopped back down into his chair.

"Madame Nadine. The answer to your prayers. So, you better start showin' some respect."

He pressed a thumb and forefinger of one hand to his eyes, closing them tiredly for a second. Paula refused to see him or take his phone calls. How could he save his marriage if she wouldn't talk to him? Despair enveloped him like a shroud. He had nowhere else to turn.

When he unshuttered his eyes, Madame Nadine patted his hand compassionately. He could swear he felt a tingling sensation where her skin brushed his.

"Tell me what happened, and let's see what we can do," she advised and lit another stinking cigarette.

Nick surprised himself by spilling his guts, giving her a brief capsule of his problem, finally ending, "So, even though Paula and I have been separated for a year, the divorce doesn't become final until next Wednesday."

"How long you been married?"

"Five years."

"Why did you split?"

"She left me," he admitted bleakly.

"And you just let her go? And you waited till now to try to get her back?" She looked at him as if he was the most brainless, ass-backwards blockhead in the world.

He was. It must show on his face.

"Just like a man. Dumber'n a doornail." She made a tsking sound of disapproval. "Do you love her?"

His throat closed over, and he had trouble speaking. Finally, he answered in a raspy voice, "Yes."

"And does she still love you?"

"Yes . . . no . . . damned if I know." He blinked rapidly, feeling his eyes begin to water. It must be the damn cigarette smoke. "Paula said that in the end love wasn't enough."

Madame Nadine nodded as if she understood perfectly. He wished he did.

"And now you want her back?"

"Desperately."

"Desperate is good." She ground her butt into an ashtray and studied the cloudy fish bowl, waving her long fingers over it with a practiced flourish. Then she raised her two hands in a *voilà* fashion. "It's simple."

"What's simple?" he asked, frowning. Had he missed something here? Maybe his brain was becoming numb from nicotine and cat breath.

"All you need to do is find your wife's heart craving."

Some memory flickered at the back of Nick's mind. Hadn't that psycho shrink on *The Woman's Edge* said something about men needing to discover what women craved? And, holy cow, the last time he'd seen Paula, she'd said he didn't have a clue as to her *cravings.*

"Heart craving? What the hell is a heart craving?"

"That's for you to discover," Madame Nadine said with a mysterious smile. Then she added dismissively, "That'll be twenty dollars. Shut the door on your way out."

Stunned, Nick watched as Madame Nadine waddled toward a beaded curtain on the other side of the room.

"But I don't understand. What kind of craving? For food? Like chocolate? Or sex? Or kids? What?"

But Madame Nadine was gone. The only thing left was her cigarette smoke—and about two zillion cat hairs on his dark trousers.

And the words, "Heart craving, heart craving, heart craving . . ." echoing in Nick's puzzled brain.

When dumb gets dumber . . .

THREE HOURS LATER, Nick was at the bookstore in the mall, doing another really dumb thing.

He'd decided to seek some reference materials.

When the salesclerk stepped away for a moment, he punched "craving" into the computer, and about two hundred entries came up, most of them in the "human sexuality" section. He wondered idly if that was different from the "unhuman sexuality" section.

So, the craving thing did refer to sex, after all. Well, he could handle that.

Not that he didn't know his way around the block, and then some. And not that he and Paula had ever had sex problems. But . . . *Hmmm,* maybe there was something he'd been missing all these years. Or, rather, something she'd been missing.

Women were always examining things to death—reading how-to books, trying to make their relationships better. They watched too much Dr. Sheila, in his opinion.

But he had an open mind. Maybe something new had been invented in the sex department recently that he hadn't heard about yet.

And, frankly, he was willing to try anything at this point. *Anything.* Yeah, he was cool with this stuff. He was an open-minded guy. He was willing to learn.

Aliens must have stolen his brain.

Still, Nick gave himself a mental push and headed toward the sex books.

An hour later, a dozen books lay at his feet, and Nick was bug-eyed and gape-mouthed with amazement. "Who reads all this stuff?" he muttered.

"My wife," a skinny guy of about ninety answered with a groan. His trousers were hiked up practically to his armpits, and four inches of white socks showed at the ankles. "Lorna—that's my honey—Lorna says she wants to spice up our lives. I think she's tryin' to kill me." He grinned with lewd satisfaction.

"Get outta here!"

"It's the truth." The gray-haired codger pulled a paperback from the shelf and handed it to Nick. "This is Lorna's favorite."

Nick turned the slim volume over in his hands and read the title aloud: *"How to Make Your Baby's Motor Hum When Her Engine Needs a Tune-Up."*

"The diagrams are pretty good, I must say." The old coot winked suggestively.

God! Against his better judgment, Nick flicked through the book till he came to the illustrations. Turning his head this way and that, he tried to figure out just where the "spark plug" was on this particular model.

"I think you have it upside down," his newfound friend informed him.

"I don't believe this," Nick said when he finally figured out the drawings.

"I'm partial to the chapter on lube jobs."

"Did you get a look at this dipstick?" Nick exclaimed, with a low whistle. "This guy must need a wheelbarrow to haul his equipment around."

"Lorna calls me Mr. Eveready—"

Nick slanted him an incredulous look.

"—but, I must say, that fella musta invented the expression 'hung like a horse.'"

Nick slammed the book shut with disgust and put it back on the shelf. Then he gathered up the pile of books at his feet, wanting to put as much space as possible between himself and this old-age pervert.

Just before he turned away, the guy added, with a chuckle, "And, I must say, the book has good advice on how to prime her starter."

Yep, I'm going off the deep end.

"Was that guy bothering you?" a teenage girl at the checkout asked as he stacked the twelve books he'd chosen on the counter. "The manager says he's harmless, but I think he's a pre-vert. Do you want us to call security?"

Nick shook his head with amusement. "Nah, he's okay."

Cracking her chewing gum loudly, the girl began to call out his purchases as she rang them up on the register, *out loud*, in a grating, singsong voice.

"*Women's Sexual Fantasies,* $4.95."

"Miss, do you think it's necessary—"

"*Two-hour Orgasms,* $10.99."

"Can you keep your voice down?"

"Huh?" She stared at him blankly, then went on, "*The All-Time, Most Spectacular Sexual Position in the World,* $34.50. Criminey! $34.50? I hope it's worth it."

"I hope so, too," Nick murmured.

"*Women Who Ejaculate,* $15.95."

The man in line behind Nick craned his neck over his shoulder and whispered, "Where'd you get *that* one?"

Nick pointed, and the man, along with two others, left the line and headed back toward the section on human sexuality.

"Listen, can you just hurry this up?"

Ignoring him, the girl yelled to a clerk on the other side of the store, at least a mile away, "Hey, Hank, can you look up the price on this one? *G-Spots and Love Knots.*"

Every single person in the store turned to look at him. Nick thought he'd like to put a knot in the big-mouth's tongue.

That night, Nick ordered pizza and sat down in his living room, surrounded by his purchases, planning a long night of "research." He was going to save his marriage or die trying.

The high school student who delivered his pizza an hour later scanned the room while Nick dug in his pockets for a tip. The kid snickered over the titles, boasting, "I know everything in these books."

"Yeah! You wish!"

The teenaged Casanova picked up one paperback, exclaiming, "Hey, I read this one. *A Thousand Ways to Kiss Your Lover.*"

"Go away," Nick said, shoving the money in his hand. First, he got advice from Gypsy Rose Wacko, then a senior citizen, now a pimply-faced adolescent.

Walking away, the know-it-all called over his shoulder with a laugh, "You oughta try the slide kiss. The women melt every time."

"You wouldn't know melt if it hit you in the face." Nick slammed the door shut. "Smart-ass," he added to the closed door.

Then he couldn't resist. He picked up the book in question, turned to the index, and moved his fingertip until he found "slide kiss." He read the brief chapter. *Wow!* A few moments later, he added "slide kiss" to the list on his notepad.

It was midnight before Nick finished the last book. He studied the voluminous notes he'd taken and saw a common thread in many of the books. In fact, he'd written an exact quote from one of the texts: *In their hearts, many women crave sexual fantasy.*

Hearts. Crave. Sexual Fantasy.

Hell, that was a definition for heart craving if he'd ever heard one.

Nick leaned back in his chair, crossed his hands behind his neck, and grinned. He had the solution to his problem.

Paula didn't stand a chance.

Chapter Three

Day Two
She's not missing him at all. Yeah, right! . . .

PAULA KEPT GLANCING toward the entrance of the diner, half expecting Nick to stroll in. She'd avoided him all last night and today, but she suspected he wouldn't give up easily.

She took another sip of coffee and scrutinized the woman sitting across the table, her good friend, Kahlita Simmons. The short, energetic black woman had slicked-back hair and horn-rimmed glasses that said a lot about her no-nonsense attitude toward life. Paula needed some no-nonsense advice on how to handle Nick's persistence.

Paula peeked at her watch anxiously. "I only have ten more minutes until my appointment with my lawyer."

"You're signing the papers today?"

Paula nodded. "Nick refuses to sign the ones that were served on him yesterday."

"Skip says he's acting crazy." Kahlita was engaged to Skip Bratton, a Newark police officer and a good friend of his.

"I know. He called at least ten times last night and left the most touching messages on my answering machine. I can't listen without crying."

"Paula, the man clearly loves you. And you love him. Isn't there any chance you can work this out?"

"No. I wish there was. Nick and I have been separated this past year, but you know, Kahlita, it's not the first time we've split. And I can't tell you how many times we've tried to work it out. Counseling. Separations. Arguments. Over and over. The man just can't change. He wants to, I think. And he tries, but he just can't change."

"And you can't live with him the way he is?"

"Could you? He's obsessed."

"There are a lot of women who would grab him in a nano-second. In fact, Skip fixed him up one night with . . ." Her words trailed off as she saw what must look like horror on Paula's face. "Oh, God, I'm sorry. I didn't think—I mean, I thought you knew."

"Nick's been dating?" she asked in a shaky voice. "Who?"

"Well, not exactly dating. See, Skip fixed him up with this stripper—"

"Nick went out with a stripper?"

"No, but Skip introduced him to one, and she's only a stripper on the side. Actually, Laura Bishop—her stage name is Jezebel—attends Harvard Med School. Anyhow, before he even finished one drink, Nick went to the men's room and never came back. He told Skip later that she was too mud-ugly for him." Kahlita laughed softly at some memory. "Skip told me that Laura is a former runner-up for Miss New Jersey."

Paula shouldn't have been relieved, but she was.

"And Lizzie Phillips, that new police trainee, has had the hots for Nick for months. Guar-an-teed, the ink won't be dry on the divorce papers before she launches a frontal attack. And believe me, she could do it with those bosoms of hers." Kahlita put two cupped hands in front of her chest to demonstrate.

Paula had met Lizzie, and she was actually a very nice, very attractive young woman. Her heart ached to think that Nick would soon be free to date other women, even if he hadn't already. Then she glanced up at Kahlita with suspicion. "I know what you're doing. You're trying to make me jealous so I'll get back with Nick."

Kahlita ducked her head sheepishly.

"If I thought there was even the remotest chance of Nick changing, I'd be back in his arms in a flash. It just isn't going to happen." She sighed deeply with resignation and stood. Shifting her shoulder bag into place, she laid some money on the table and added, "It's time to get on with my life. And Nick, too. I'm sure that once we're divorced, I'll start to get over him. All the old cravings will go away, eventually."

Brave words, she thought, as she entered her lawyer's building down the street, *but I'm deathly afraid Nick is the only man I'll ever crave.*

He gave new meaning to the word "frisking" . . .

TWO HOURS LATER, Paula was cruising down the highway, dabbing at her eyes with a tissue. In the orange glow of the setting sun, she could see the final legal papers she'd picked up at her lawyer's office sitting on the passenger seat. A reminder of everything wonderful she'd had in her life—and lost.

Oh, Nick! Why can't you change?

Sighing with regret, Paula glanced idly in the rearview mirror. And saw the blinking red-and-blue light.

Immediately, she checked her speedometer and groaned. She was going fifteen miles over the speed limit.

"Great! That's all I need today. My life is going down the toilet, and now I get a speeding ticket, besides. What next?"

The berm of the highway was too narrow, so she veered off at the next exit and drove a short distance down a rural road before she could find a large enough area to pull over. The marked police car followed close behind.

Muttering with self-disgust at her carelessness, she had her license, registration, and insurance papers ready before the uniformed cop walked up. Rolling down her window, she handed him the cards.

"Where's the fire, lady?" a gruff voice asked.

"I wasn't really going *that* fast, Officer. Only—"

"Step out of the car, ma'am," he cut her off in a stern, muffled voice. Paula glanced up, but all she could see was a strong male jaw and a flash of suntanned skin, shaded by dark sunglasses and a hat. Before she could look closer, the tall, rangy figure turned his back on her and began examining her cards. Over his wide shoulders, he asked, in an extremely deep, gravelly voice, "Is that Miss or Mrs. DiCello?"

She swallowed hard. With the divorce pending, she suddenly

realized . . . oh, Lord . . . in six more days, would she be Miss once again? She wasn't sure, but for now, she replied, "Mrs."

He nodded, as if pleased by her answer. "Any outstanding warrants?" His head was averted, looking down at the small clipboard in front of him as he wrote.

"No."

"Last speeding ticket?"

"Two months ago, but I can explain. It was a reduced speed zone and—"

"Save it for the judge, sweetheart."

She thought she heard a smile in his voice. He probably heard hundreds of excuses every day. In fact, Nick once told her about a lady who, when caught speeding, said she was ovulating and had to get home to make love with her husband before her body temperature changed. She smiled to herself as she recalled how she and Nick had spent that afternoon in bed as well, making slow, delicious love. And definitely raising some body temperatures.

There she went, thinking about Nick again. Paula forcibly brought her thoughts back to the present.

"Drug convictions?"

"Absolutely not."

"Prostitution?"

"I resent this questioning. I just came from my lawyer's office. I'm going to call him right now." She turned, about to open the car door and get her cellular phone.

"Put your hands on the roof of the car and spread your legs," the police officer snapped.

"Not on your life—*oompf!*" The cop had put his palm on the center of her back and shoved her up against the car. Her breasts, covered by a silk tank top, pressed into the driver's window. Her belly, under a long, gauzy skirt, flattened against the warm metal of the door. "Hey! Who do you think you are? You can't do this."

"Wanna bet?" With one deft movement, he forced her arms up and over the top of the car. A knee between the back of her legs quickly separated and spread her legs.

This can't be happening to me. Not after all the years that Nick warned me about all the dangers out here and the precautions to take. She prayed that another car would drive by soon, take in the situation, and stop. But she realized with dismay that not one car had approached the lonely spot thus far.

The officer's large hands brushed over the filmy fabric covering her buttocks, and alarm bells went off in her head.

"Is this the kind of outfit a *lady* wears to her lawyer's?"

"That's none of your business."

His hands continued on a slow, frisking path along her sides. Over her waist. The sides of her breasts. Her armpits. And higher, over her shoulders and along her arms.

"What do you think you're doing?" she cried out in panic. She tried, futilely, to squirm free from his imprisoning arms and legs.

"Full body search."

"For what?" Skepticism and outrage had turned her voice shrill.

He hesitated, then murmured, "Contraband."

"I'm going to report you," she warned.

"Go right ahead."

"This is not standard operating procedure. Believe me, I know lots of cops."

He chuckled. "I'll bet you do, honey."

Paula felt his breath against the back of her neck. The hard ridge between his legs pressed against her bottom. The fragrance of a woodsy aftershave drifted around her. Hauntingly familiar, yet different. Evocative of forbidden, secret delights.

The back of her neck prickled as an elusive memory tugged at the back of her mind.

Paula pressed her cheek against the roof of the car and spread the palms of her outstretched arms. Perhaps if she didn't struggle, this whole sordid experience would be over in moments and she could just go home.

She watched, mesmerized, as the long fingers of his hands skimmed the surface of her bare skin from shoulders to elbows to wrists. For a second, the hands paused, then lay over hers, gently, dwarfing them with their size. Dark skin against light. A leather watchband. A gold wedding band.

Wedding band!

Paula blinked and looked again at the hand that rested intimately over hers, then moved to the side. Two gold wedding bands, side by side. Identical.

Tears filled her eyes as recognition hit her.

She struggled in earnest now. "Let me go."

"Never."

"You bastard!" Paula let loose with a number of expletives then, too furious to curb her tongue. She couldn't stop looking at the two matching wedding rings.

The cop just laughed softly with appreciation. "I love it when you talk dirty, honey."

"Is it worth losing your job?"

"Yes," he said without hesitation.

Paula's heart skipped a beat at that one simple word. What did he mean?

Then she couldn't think at all.

Outrageously, the policeman swept the long strands of her hair behind her ear, exposing her neck to the nuzzling of his warm lips. He bit the lobe of her ear, softly, and inserted the tip of his tongue in its crevices.

"Just what kind of search is this?" she choked out.

"Cavity search," he growled—a hungry, masculine sound, both threatening and tantalizing—then traced the sensitive whorls with expert precision.

Paula groaned. Sweet, erotic tingles spread from the teasing movements of his tongue in her ear to her breasts, which swelled and peaked. A dull ache began to grow at the vee of her legs.

She was no longer frightened of a strange cop. She was frightened of herself and her unwilling surrender to the dangerous, erotic fantasy.

"You're going to get arrested," she gasped as his fingers found her nipples and played with them.

"Probably." He didn't sound at all concerned.

Impatiently, he tugged her shirt from the waistband of her

skirt, and his hands moved up over her bare skin to her lace-covered breasts, molding them to fit his palms, tugging at the nipples, rolling them between his fingers. All the time, he whispered sexy, explicit words in her ears about what he would like to do to her, what he intended to do to her.

"O-o-oh!"

Paula's thighs grew heavy and weak. She almost swooned with the sheer agonizing pleasure that rolled over her body in waves.

This was some wanton creature Paula did not recognize. It couldn't be she, undulating her hips against his hardening erection, arching her back to give him greater access to her aching breasts, her flat stomach, and lower.

She'd been so lonely since Nick had left. Yesterday's lovemaking in the shower had only whetted a hunger she'd thought long dead. That was the only excuse for her body's betrayal.

Determined male hands bunched the fabric of her skirt in gathering fists, lifting the hem higher and higher, up to the sides of her bikini panties. Then, in one hard jerk, they ripped away both sides of her underpants. The silky fabric fell to the ground, exposing her still widespread legs to exploring fingers.

One hand moved back up to her breasts, fingering them lightly. The other hand found her wet heat.

"My God!" he exclaimed behind her, his lips pressed against the pulse beat in her neck. Then, "Sweet. Oh, baby, you are so sweet."

She almost fainted. Then she bucked back against him, trying to break free, to no avail.

He nipped her shoulder with his teeth, asserting his controlled aggression.

She pressed her forehead against the car roof, barely able to stand as his expert fingers found her pleasure points and played a tortuous game of fluttery music.

Just then she heard a car motor approaching.

"Holy hell! Don't move," he ordered, shielding her body with his own as the pickup truck slowed, then continued down the highway past them.

Paula barely noticed. And yelling for help was the last thing on her mind.

She started to look back at him over her shoulder.

The rasp of a zipper stopped her.

Then her hips were being lifted and tilted backward into the cradle of a hard male body. Her sandaled feet barely touched the road.

In one long stroke, he entered her, and Paula couldn't suppress the keen of pure ecstasy. Her body welcomed him with rippling convulsions that seemed to make him grow inside her, harder and thicker, filling her to excess. And more.

He moaned low in his throat. A raw, savage noise.

When her first climax passed, he lifted her hips higher, penetrating her even deeper. Then he began to move. Long, slow thrusts, accompanied by seductive murmurs. Forbidden words. Scandalous thoughts. Fantasies, imagined but never spoken aloud.

"Do you like that, sweetheart?"

"Oh . . . oh, yes!"

"And that?"

"Please . . ."

"Can I touch you there?"

She put a restraining hand on his wrist, shocked, then lifted it in sweet, reckless surrender.

"Would you like to be handcuffed?"

"I don't know. Maybe."

"You're my prisoner."

"Yes."

"You can't escape."

"I know."

"You have to do what I say. Everything."

Hot, sensual images flashed through her mind. Wicked. Dark. Taboo. She licked her lips. "And if I don't?"

"I'll stop. Do you want me to stop?"

"Never."

When his strokes turned short and hard, Paula became

mindless, incapable of thought or talk. A hot tide of molten sensation engulfed her. She fought her orgasm, and raced toward it, out of control.

The twilight air resonated with the sounds of crickets from the nearby woods, and heavy breathing. His and hers. Melded. In rhythm.

When the final climax came—a shattering explosion of the senses—he drew back one last time and slammed into her, his thighs braced rigid with tension, the sinews of his arms roped with muscles. They cried out their release together and gasped for breath as her searing sheath continued to caress him with smaller and smaller spasms until, whimpering, she could bear no more. And he wilted with the intensity of his release.

Softly, he kissed the back of her neck.

After a long moment, he pulled out of her and let her feet slide to the ground. But his arms continued to hold her from behind, one around her waist, the other gently stroking her arms and shoulders and hair. She could feel his heart thudding wildly against her back.

Finally, he turned her in his arms, still pressed against the car. He must have removed his hat and sunglasses before making love with her. His short-clipped hair was as thick and black as a moonless night.

His eyes held hers for a long, poignant moment in question, perhaps wondering if she was angry or pleased. Blue pools of passion surrounded by thick, black spidery lashes. So beautiful.

Slowly, he lowered his head. With tenderest care, his full lips brushed her mouth. A pleading caress. No demands here. A lover's kiss.

Then he drew back and grazed his knuckles along her jaw and tilted her chin upward.

Paula could see the sexual satisfaction in his misty eyes and parted lips. And she saw the silent sadness on his face, as well.

"Come home, Paula," he pleaded huskily. "Please, come home."

Chapter Four

Baby, come back . . .

TIME SEEMED TO stand still as Nick waited for Paula's answer. Surely, they would reconcile after what had just happened between them.

He couldn't believe his plan had gone so well. Hell, satisfying this heart-craving business was going to be a snap. And more damn pleasure than he'd ever imagined in his hottest wet dreams.

Now, all he had to do was get Paula to come home with him, and he'd spend the rest of his life fulfilling every sexual fantasy—every heart craving—she could ever have. And then some.

Who was he kidding? He'd forgotten his plan the moment she'd stepped from the car. He couldn't have stopped himself from touching her if his life depended on it. He'd been celibate for so long—a year, in fact, until yesterday.

And he had to admit, she'd surprised the spit out of him. He had never been so demanding in the four years they'd been together. Or suggested such exotic sexual activity. And, hot damn, she'd liked it. A lot.

He brushed several strands of silky auburn hair off her face, and she swatted his hand away. That was his first clue that fantasy island was fast becoming a mirage.

The second clue came right after that, when he rubbed the pad of his thumb over her passion-swollen lips, and she bit him, hard.

"Ouch! Why'd you do that?" He stepped back, sucking on the sore appendage. With a sigh, he then adjusted himself inside his pants and zipped up. The cold, angry glitter in her green eyes did not bode well for sexual seconds.

"Are you crazy?" she lashed out, smoothing down her silk tank top. Her still-aroused nipples stood out like sentinels, and he couldn't help the slow grin that pulled at his lips.

She looked down and grunted with self-disgust, then folded her arms across her chest. "You are a toad."

"Yeah. You wanna check out my warts?" He reached out for her, but she ducked under his arms. "Or we could play leap frog."

"Aaarrgh! Would you stop kidding around?" She reached down with a groan of dismay and picked up her torn panties, stuffing them into her skirt pocket. Turning back to him, she asked tiredly, "What did you hope to accomplish here—no, let me guess. You figured a quick screw on the side of the road, and I'd drop the divorce petition. God, you must have a low opinion of me."

He cringed at her vulgar assessment. "We made love, Paula. And you're just mad because you enjoyed it so much."

"I did not," she said, raising her chin defensively.

"Liar."

"And stop grinning at me."

He shrugged and grinned even wider.

"You are such a rat."

He jiggled his eyebrows. "And that would make you the cheese. Would you like me to eat—"

"Don't even say it!" She began pacing back and forth along the length of the car. "Nick, you caught me in a weak moment, but it's not going to happen again. Ever! You've got to give up. It's over."

"No. No, it's not. If you'd just come home, we could talk—"

"Like we 'talked' just now? Like we 'talked' in the shower yesterday?"

"Why are you being so difficult?"

"Why can't you understand that our marriage is dead? And sex can't resurrect it."

He closed his eyes briefly on that painful thought.

"What are you doing in uniform anyhow? You haven't been

in uniform since you made detective ten years ago. I'm surprised it still fits."

"It didn't," he admitted sheepishly. "Skip loaned me his."

"Skip? Oh, you are too much! Dragging other people into our affairs." She blushed as a sudden thought occurred to her. "You didn't tell him why you wanted the uniform, did you?"

"Nah, it's our secret. Listen, honey, it's getting dark. Let's go back to our apartment—I mean, your place—and talk. I promise I won't touch you again. Unless you want me to."

She flashed him a look of utter disbelief. "I'm not going anywhere with you, Nick. And we're getting a divorce six days from now." Tears filled her eyes as she gazed up at him bleakly.

"I love you, Paula. Doesn't that count for anything?"

"Oh, Nick. Of course, it does. But we've been over this a hundred times before. Your love suffocates me."

He flinched at her harsh words. "I can change."

"No, you can't. You've tried. Many times. But you can't stop smothering me with your obsessiveness."

"I only want to keep you safe. What's wrong with that?"

"Nick, I hated that high-rise prison we lived in."

"It was a maximum security complex," he corrected. "That's why we moved there in the first place. And I got us another place, just like you wanted."

"No, Nick, like *you* wanted. Not me." She shook her head wearily. "A low-rise apartment building with bars on the windows is not my idea of home."

He drew himself up, affronted. "They aren't bars. They're security grills."

"Why couldn't we have lived in the suburbs? All I wanted was a little house with a backyard and an apple tree."

"Uh-uh. Too unsafe, especially close to the city."

She made a clucking sound of disgust. "And my car? I asked for a Volkswagen convertible, and you bought me a Volvo sedan."

"Honey, soft-top cars are an invitation for burglars. You could be attacked at a stoplight, even with the doors locked."

"And Gonzo! Lord, I asked for a cocker spaniel, and you

gave me a small horse."

"A German shepherd is one of the best guard dogs." He looked wounded at her lack of appreciation. "I thought you liked Gonzo."

"I love Gonzo. *Now.* But he's not what I wanted."

"So, you're pissed off because of a house, a car, and a damned dog?"

"Aaarrgh! Listen to me for once, you stubborn fool. Those things were just bricks in the wall you were putting up day by day. What hurt the most the last couple of years was your refusal to talk about your work."

He braced himself, knowing what was coming next.

"I had no idea what kind of cases you handled. Sometimes you were so angry, or sad, and you kept it all inside."

"Paula, I'm surrounded by muck in my job. The dregs of humanity. Believe me, you don't want to know about some of the things I witness."

"How do you know what I want, you blockhead? God, you're impossible! And my job—you refused to listen—oh, I give up!" She threw her hands up in the air. "We've been over this a million times."

Nick's pride tempted him to turn on his heel and say, "To hell with it, then." But he couldn't give up without one last salvo, "Don't you love me anymore?"

She averted her eyes.

"Tell me. Say the words, 'I don't love you, Nick.'"

A single tear slid down her cheek, and she wiped at it angrily.

He felt like a fist was squeezing his heart.

"You know I can't. Not yet," she said on a sob. "But I'm going to learn to stop. And finalizing the divorce is the first step." With determination, she opened her car door and slid behind the steering wheel.

"I have six more days to convince you otherwise," he shouted through the closed window, with equal determination.

"Give it up, Nick. All I crave now is . . ."

Crave? He couldn't hear the rest of her words as she revved the motor and shot out onto the highway. At first, his shoulders slumped with defeat. But then, in the wake of skidding gravel and exhaust fumes, he noticed the oddest thing growing along the road.

A lone sunflower.

Day Three
Bad boys come in all sizes . . .

Nick finished booking the three teenage boys for burglary, carrying an unlicensed firearm, resisting arrest, and possession of narcotics.

"Man, you gonna lock us up again?" the freckle-faced kid with the nose ring whined.

"You bet your stupid ass, I am, Peterman. And this time, I'm asking the judge to send you to Stonegate."

"I ain't goin' to no juvie hall again. Betcha my momma'll have me outta here by tomorrow."

"Not if I can help it! When are you guys gonna learn?" Nick's contemptuous glare took in Peterman, as well as his two buddies, Casale and Lewis. They all wore T-shirts proclaiming the name of their gang, "Blades."

"Learn what?" Casale asked angrily. "You make me puke. You sit in your lily-white houses in your lily-white neighborhood. Whaddayou know what it's like in our hood, Po-lice-man?" His intelligent eyes bespoke a deep rage—one Nick, unfortunately, understood too well.

"I know that your way is a dead-end street, *Richard*."

Nick saw Casale grit his teeth at the use of his given name. Somehow, the anonymity of surnames suited these street gangs better. Growing up, Nick doubted any one ever knew his first name. It was always just, "Hey, DiCello!"

Patiently, in a softer tone of voice, he informed Casale, "Richie, I was born in your hood . . . Patterson Street. I lived in the same project you do, maybe even the same unit." At the look of disbelief on the kid's face, he asked, "Do the halls still smell like spaghetti sauce and urine all the time?"

Casale blinked with surprise. Then he sneered, "We got us a *crew-say-dah* here, boys. A real Deputy Do-Right. There ain't nothin' worse than a reformed bad boy."

Nick made a blowing noise of exasperation. What was the use? "You do know that the captain wants you guys charged as adults this time?"

A brief spark of fear appeared in Casale's brilliant blue eyes before he masked it with the usual bravado. Of the three, this kid had the most potential to pull himself out of the ghetto dung heap. But he probably wouldn't.

Nick filled in the last of the forms, then motioned for the patrolman at the door to lead them away. Handcuffed and shackled, the trio shuffled down the hallway to the holding pen, arrogant and unremorseful. They knew the way with their eyes closed.

Nick felt a twinge of pity for the stupid kids. Hell, they were only fourteen years old. Yeah, fourteen going on forty! And with rap sheets to rival those of the hardest criminals.

Any sympathy he might have considered died when Lewis looked back over his shoulder and called out, "I'm gonna get you, DiCello. I'm sick of you jerks pickin' me up. Watch your back, you sonofabitch. I got a bullet with your name on it."

Lewis was the most incorrigible gang member he'd encountered in the last few years—a vicious, surly punk with a chip on his shoulder the size of a tombstone.

"I'm shivering in my boots," he snapped back.

"Yeah, well, how 'bout your old lady? You even got a chick, you fag?" Lewis asked.

Nick made a low hissing sound.

Seeing that he'd found Nick's vulnerable spot, the creep laughed evilly—how could a kid so young be so evil?—and spelled out graphically, in filthy gutter language, what he could do to Nick's "old lady" to get back at him.

Trembling with fury, Nick started after the hoodlum. But Skip stepped up to him and put a restraining hand on his shoulder. "Let him go, Nick. They all make threats like that. He's just a punk with an attitude."

As a final insult, all three delinquents flicked their middle fingers at him.

Nick pressed his forehead against the cold concrete wall, inhaling and exhaling deeply.

And Paula wonders why I don't want to talk about my work. Or why I'm overprotective. Hell!

Finally, his temper cooled. He looked back at Skip—a patrol officer and friend, only twenty-five years old, who worked out of the same precinct. "You off duty now?"

Skip nodded.

"How 'bout going for a beer?"

"Sounds good."

They were about to leave the building when Captain O'Malley called out, "See you tonight, DiCello. Right?" The burly Irishman smirked from ear to ear, then erupted into a deep belly laugh.

Nick felt a flush move up his neck. "Yeah, I'll be there."

"Eight o'clock. The high school gym. Don't be late." He started laughing again.

"What was that all about?" Skip asked as they walked toward his patrol car.

"I'm going to the prom."

Twerk, jerk, same thing . . .

LATER, NICK AND Skip were nursing their second beers in a neighborhood tavern.

"Stop smirkin' at me," Nick said.

"I can't help it. Geez, I just can't picture you at a prom. Do you even know how to boogie?"

"Boogie? I was thinking more along the lines of dirty danc—"

His words were interrupted by the waitress, who smiled invitingly down at Skip and asked, for the third time in a half hour, "Will there be anything else, sugar?" She totally ignored Nick.

Skip winked. "Not now, darlin'."

Smiling, Nick shook his head at his friend. "Stop flirting

with the waitresses. If Kahlita were here, she'd wring your neck. And you're not on stage now, so you have no excuse." Everywhere he went, Skip attracted women. And it wasn't just that he looked like Denzel Washington in an Arnold Schwarzenegger body. Skip exuded sexual charisma without even giving it a thought. *Hmmm. Maybe Skip can give me a little advice.*

"Maybe you ought to moonlight, too," Skip suggested. "Might learn a few tricks to lure Paula back."

Now that was hitting too close to home. Nick winced. "Me? A male stripper? Hardly. Besides, if you're not careful, the captain's gonna hear about your nightclub act. Do you wanna get fired?"

Skip shrugged. "Maybe it would be for the best. The money's better, for sure. And, no kidding . . . Sal is looking for someone to replace Lee as the Indian in the line-up. Lee got moved up to detective. He's working night shift now and had to quit."

Nick choked on his beer. "Lee Chin was stripping? As an Indian? Holy hell! He's Chinese."

Skip grinned. "Yeah, but the women didn't seem to notice his face. They were lookin' a little . . . lower. Then, too, he can flex his buttocks. I don't suppose you can do the twerk."

"The who?"

"The twerk. It's a dance move where you squat down and spread your knees, then vibrate your butt cheeks real fast." He stood and demonstrated. At the look of horror on Nick's face, he remarked, "I guess not."

Smiling, Nick leaned back and sipped at his beer. "Even if I had the inclination, this aging body couldn't stand the scrutiny of a couple hundred screaming women. I could lift weights till my nose bleeds and still not look like you. Besides, I'm trying to get my wife back, and Paula's not the type to go for male strippers."

"Actually, Paula and Kahlita came to the club one night. They seemed to be having a good time." Skip raised an eyebrow knowingly.

Nick gaped at Skip's grinning face. "Not my Paula!"

"Maybe you don't know Paula as well as you think."

If they can't make love, at least they can dance . . .

PAULA HAD JUST returned to her apartment that afternoon when the doorbell rang. A delivery man stood there with a stack of boxes imprinted with the name of Macy's department store.

At first, Paula frowned with puzzlement when she opened the boxes and peeled away the tissue paper. There was a beautiful, strapless evening gown, white, embroidered with pastel flowers along the bodice and the hem of the full, frothy skirt. In addition, the other boxes contained matching sling-back high heels, sheer silk stockings, and a corsage. *A corsage?*

Paula knew, even before she read the enclosed card. *Nick.*

Sighing, she sank into an easy chair and read. "Will you be my date for the prom tonight? Love, Nick."

Oh, what a low blow! Nick knew that she'd never gone to a dance in her high school days. She'd attended a private Catholic girls' school in the suburbs, which held no such frivolous events. And she'd told him once that it was a part of growing up she'd wanted to experience, but had missed. And Nick had remembered that!

Just then, she noticed the red light blinking on her answering machine.

The first call was from her lawyer, reminding her of their court date next Wednesday. *Oh, God! Only five days away. I feel like I have a time bomb ticking away inside my heart.*

Next, her mother invited her to use the beach house at Long Beach Island for the next few weeks. She and her dad planned to visit some friends in Florida.

Finally, Nick's voice came on.

"Paula, don't hang up. Just hear me out. Please, honey, go to the prom with me tonight. Captain O'Malley's daughter is graduating, and they need extra chaperons." She heard the chuckle in his voice. *His deep, wonderful voice. The voice she might not be hearing again after this week.* She closed her eyes briefly against the soul-searing pain.

"I know it's not the same, going as chaperons instead of high school seniors. But we could pretend. And, Paula"—his voice deepened with emotion—"I never told you . . . but I never went to a prom, either. And . . . and I really, *really* would like to experience it with you. It's only one night, babe."

"Oh, Nick," Paula murmured, pressing his note against her heart, "why can't you just give it up? Our marriage is over."

"Honey, I know our marriage is over . . ." he said.

She jerked to attention. Criminy, was he reading her mind now?

". . . but we can still be friends, can't we? And I promise . . . I swear to God . . . I won't jump your bones."

She smiled grimly. *But how do I stop myself from jumping yours?*

"I'll pick you up at eight. Okay?"

Paula felt her resistance crumbling. She wanted to go to a prom. More important, she wanted to go to a prom *with Nick*. But she shouldn't. If she were smart, she'd take this beautiful dress and send it back to the store. She'd call Nick and tell him she couldn't go.

"Don't try to call me back, hon. I'm driving Skip down to the nightclub. He's gonna teach me how to be an Indian strip dancer. You oughta see me swing my . . . uh, tomahawk."

Her mouth dropped open with incredulity.

"And twerk."

"Whaaat? You?"

"Just kidding."

She laughed, despite herself.

"Bye, honey, see you later."

She heard him drop the phone with a loud clatter and a sharp expletive. Then, just before her answering machine clicked off, she thought he muttered something about heart cravings giving him heartburn.

Chapter Five

You had to give the guy credit for trying . . .

"THIS IS NOT a date, Nick," she said that evening as they were driving to the Montclair high school.

"Right," he agreed, too readily.

Nick flashed her a dazzling smile before turning his attention back to maneuvering the car through the busy parkway traffic.

Just his nearness overwhelmed her. He looked so handsome. She'd never seen him in a tux before. She had to admit that accompanying him to this prom, no matter how foolish, was worth it, just to see him in formal attire. Forget about *Playgirl* centerfolds. Nick in a black tuxedo was sexier than any of the nude models, hands down.

"And we're not getting back together," she asserted. "The divorce still goes through on Wednesday."

His strong hands, lean-fingered and capable, gripped the steering wheel with a vengeance, turning the knuckles white. Staring straight ahead, he agreed, "Right." But there was a gritty tone to his voice.

"And you are most definitely not going to 'jump my bones.'"

A grin tugged at his firm lips. "Right."

"No hanky-panky."

He gave her a sideways glance of amusement. "Define hanky-panky."

She laughed. This was the old Nick—the one she'd fallen in love with five years ago. What had changed him into the somber, overly protective, possessive, withdrawn male of recent years? She remembered their early days together when he'd been just like he was now—teasing, carefree, irresistibly charming, devastatingly attractive, sexy as hell. *Oh, Lord, I am playing with fire. This is a big mistake.*

"Did you groan?" he asked.

"No, it was probably the wind." She tossed her head back and let her hair blow in the breeze. "Who lent you the Volkswagen convertible?"

At first, he didn't answer, and she sat up straighter, suddenly suspicious. "Nick?"

"Okay, I bought it for you, but don't get your hackles up. The dealer said you could bring the Volvo in for the trade-in next week. It's not as if it's a gift or anything."

"You traded in my car?" she sputtered. "I don't believe you! You actually traded in my car without asking me?"

"Geez, Paula, you said I never listen to you. Just yesterday, *remember*, you complained that you always wanted a VW convertible, and I got you a Volvo."

Tears of frustration smarted her eyes. "You just don't get it, do you, Nick?"

He pulled to a stop in the parking lot of the high school, flipped off the ignition, and turned toward her, clearly aggravated. "What now? No matter what I do these days, I piss you off. I just can't seem to please you, no matter what. You want a car, you don't want a car. You want a dog, you don't want a dog. You want to move, you don't want to move. Make up your mind."

"Oh, you are a real piece of work, DiCello. Do you really believe our marriage went to hell in a hand-basket over a stupid car? Or a mangy mutt?"

"God knows! Because I sure as hell don't." He got out of the car and stomped around to her side, opening her door with a jerk, almost pulling it off its hinges. When she got out and stood before him, he slammed it shut with a bang. He breathed in and out several times to calm his temper, just the way he always did. Then his shoulders slumped. "C'mon, Paula, let's forget the fighting . . . just for tonight."

She wanted to reach up and smooth the frown from his

suntanned forehead, to brush his unruly ebony hair off his face, to erase the look of hurt in his eyes. But all she could do was agree. "Okay. Friends . . . for tonight."

He muttered something foul under his breath about friends.

"What?"

"I said, let's not fight. I didn't say I wanted to be your BFF or whatever you call it." With a grumble of disgust, he took her elbow, leading her toward the school entrance. "And don't be surprised if that VW convertible is stolen while we're inside."

Dancing the night away . . .

MIDNIGHT CAME too quickly. Time to go home. But Nick didn't want the night to end. "One more dance?" he asked.

"Definitely," Paula said with a sigh. Like a cloud of her lemony perfume, she drifted into his arms, which encircled her waist. Leaning her head back, she looked up at him dreamily.

She had curled her shoulder-length auburn hair so that it looked expertly mussed and incredibly wanton. Her green eyes appeared misty.

"Thank you, Nick, for a wonderful, wonderful evening. I haven't had this much fun in a long, long time."

"The pleasure was mine, babe," he said, pulling her closer. The band was playing a slow, steamy backdrop to the singer's not-so-bad rendition of that old Meatloaf song, "I Would Do Anything For Love."

That was for sure!

"I think your captain got a big kick out of you being at a prom," she said with a laugh. Her breath tickled his ear and sent slingshots of white-hot messages to other important parts of his body. "I like him—and his wife, too."

"Yeah. O'Malley's okay. His daughter was a little embarrassed to have her parents here, though."

"Wouldn't you have been, at that age?"

He stiffened with sudden memory. He knew exactly where he'd been the night of his senior prom. And it hadn't been a high school gym. More like the city hospital, watching his mother die of liver failure. Too many years of whatever cheap wine she could scrounge up with her welfare checks. And his father . . . he hadn't seen the worthless bastard since he was five years old.

"Nick . . . Nick . . . what's wrong?"

"Huh?" He forced his thoughts back to the present. Paula was staring at him with concern. "Nothing's wrong. By the way, did I tell you how beautiful you look tonight?"

"Only a hundred times."

She looked so sweet, and seductive at the same time, in the gown he'd bought for her earlier that day. The strapless top pushed her breasts up, creating a cleavage he'd have liked to sink his hands into. And the skirt billowed out like a froth of white cotton candy, brushing against his legs enticingly as they danced.

No wonder he'd been in a state of blistering half-arousal the entire night.

"You look pretty spectacular yourself, cowboy." She swayed in perfect rhythm with him to the music.

"You think so, huh?" He winked at her. "Does that mean I get to jump your bones?"

She laughed. "Not on your life!"

"How 'bout a drive before I take you home, then?"

"I don't know if that's a good idea," she said dubiously.

He didn't look forward to cramping his body into that motorized tin can, but he'd do anything to keep her at his side just a little longer.

"Aw, c'mon. We're supposed to be pretending this is our senior prom. Don't young kids go out somewhere afterwards? All-night parties. Restaurants. Movies." *Motels.*

"Well, yes, but—"

"Be a sport, Paula. Don't you *crave* a little fantasy?" *Good Lord, I hope so! If not, Madame Nadine is a gold-plated fraud, and I'm the sucker of the year.* "Besides, this might be the last time . . ." His words drifted off. He couldn't voice the possibility that this might be their last time together.

But Paula honed in on the fantasy part. "I think you gave me enough fantasy yesterday to last a lifetime." Her lips parted, reflexively, in remembrance.

You ain't seen nothin' yet, sweetheart. "Just a drive."

He got to second base . . . then struck out . . .

NICK HAD DRIVEN all the way to Sandy Hook to show her the beautiful sight of a full moon and bright stars shining on the mirrorlike surface of the ocean at low tide. But Paula wasn't fooled for one minute. He'd come here to park and neck . . . and more.

She couldn't be mad at him, though. He'd given her this magical night, a gift to make up for the past year of pain, a special way to end their marriage . . . amicably, without rancor.

They pushed their seats all the way back and arched their necks so they could gaze at the sky. Still, Nick's long legs were bent at the knees, and his tall frame spilled over onto the gear shift. He was definitely not made for a VW.

"Why are you smiling?" he asked, putting his right arm behind her seat and twirling one of her long curls around a finger.

"I was just thinking that when I asked you for a VW, I never realized that you wouldn't fit."

"Who says I don't fit?" he said, feigning affront.

"I say. Well, at least I'm safe in this cramped space. No way could two people—"

He tugged on her hair, still wrapped around his finger, and pulled her closer. Against her lips, he whispered, "Don't bet on it."

"Nick, you promised," she demurred, faintly, before his lips captured hers, sliding back and forth with exquisite care, teasing, barely touching, just sliding over the wet surface, coaxing.

Finally, she could stand no more. Putting her hands on either side of his face, she held him firmly still and pressed her lips to his.

At first, he made a low chuckling sound deep in his throat, mumbling something about chalking one up for slide kisses. Then he growled and proceeded to take charge of the kiss.

His teeth nipped at her bottom lip. When she opened her

mouth to protest, his tongue plunged deep, then withdrew. He devoured her lips in ever-changing kisses—soft, gentle, coaxing caresses, alternating with hot, bruising promises of searing passion.

Waves of longing swept over her, turning her skin hot. Her breasts grew heavy, and the vee between her legs felt molten and damp.

She moaned around his tongue.

He moaned back.

Once, he pulled away, gasping for air. "We're not going to make love," he assured her. "I'll keep my promise."

She nodded, wanting to tell him to forget his promise.

"Just a little necking," he assured her, nuzzling her cheek. "Like two teenagers after their senior prom. A little horny, but not ready to go all the way."

"Are you saying I'm horny?" she asked, trying to sound insulted.

He chucked her under the chin and grinned. "I know I'm horny as hell. Maybe you're just turned on." He put his mouth near her ear and played tongue games with its delicate crevices, whispering, "Are you turned on, babe?"

She thought about lying, then admitted, "Like an oven."

He laughed and, in one expert move, put his hands on her waist and lifted and turned her so that she lay across his lap, breast to chest. Her legs were bent and draped on the passenger seat, and her back pressed into the steering wheel, but she hardly noticed the discomfort because Nick had unzipped the back of her dress and was lowering the bodice of her strapless gown to her waist.

She objected feebly.

He inhaled sharply, and in the bright moonlight, she could see the hazy mist of want in his half-closed eyes. His parted lips looked thick and swollen from her kisses.

"Oh, Paula, honey . . ." His voice was choked with emotion as he gazed down at her, then touched her nipples lightly with the fingertips of both hands. She keened softly as ripples of intense, almost painful pleasure shot out from her breasts. She threw her head back and arched her chest forward, inviting.

"Show me," he whispered huskily.

And she drew his mouth down.

He cradled the underside of one breast in one hand, pushing upward, then took her hardened nipple, openmouthed, flicking it with his tongue until she mewled with yearning. Only then did he suckle her in earnest, hard, his cheeks flexing with the rhythm. By the time he gave equal treatment to the other breast, she was gasping for breath.

Nick seemed to have trouble breathing himself.

"So, this is necking, huh?" she teased when he finally looked up at her.

"Well, maybe we've progressed to petting," he admitted, smiling sheepishly.

"Do you suppose teenage girls do this, as well?" she asked, reaching between their bodies and running her palm over the ridge of his erection. She wanted to give as much enjoyment as he was giving her.

He groaned in sweet agony, flinging his head back against the seat, as she continued to fondle him in the way he liked best. Suddenly, he stiffened and set her back in her own seat with an abruptness that startled her.

Jerking the car door open, he walked onto the beach and bent over at the waist, clasping his thighs, inhaling and exhaling with labored breaths. Finally, he stood and just stared out over the ocean, a bleak, lonely figure.

Confused, Paula adjusted her gown and stepped out of the car. Putting her hand on his arm, she asked, "Nick, what's wrong?"

"I promised I wouldn't jump your bones tonight."

"Well, maybe . . . well, maybe I changed my mind."

"About the divorce?" he asked hopefully.

"No, of course not. Just about . . . you know."

His jaw clenched angrily. "Well, I want more than a quick lay."

"Nick, don't ruin tonight by arguing. It was a wonderful evening. I didn't know how much I had craved this kind of thing. It was like a fantasy come true."

"You craved the fantasy?" he said with decided interest, his face no longer so despondent.

"I guess I did. Deep in my heart."

He said the oddest thing then, "Thank you, Lord . . . and Madame Nadine. At least I'm on the right track."

Day Four
The things a guy will do for love . . .

"Ouch! I thought you said this wouldn't hurt."

"No, darlin', you asked me if getting a tattoo might fulfill your wife's 'heart craving,' and I said it probably wouldn't hurt. It's not the same thing."

Sitting on a high stool, Nick tried to peer back over his shoulder at Madame Nadine, who was working with concentration on his right shoulder blade. Or at least as much concentration as she could muster with that blasted cigarette hanging out of her mouth, cats meowing all over the place, and flowers sucking all the oxygen out of the air. Or did flowers give off oxygen? He couldn't remember in the midst of his pain.

"Ouch!" he said again.

"Stop moving. I can't see."

Hah! He didn't know how she could see anyhow in the glare of her bright orange dress embroidered all over with neon yellow sequined sunflowers. The broad did have a thing about sunflowers.

"Watch you don't burn me with that damn cigarette," he grumbled as her two-inch ash grazed and crumbled against the back of his neck.

Madame Nadine mumbled something that sounded an awful lot like "Up yours." But he was probably mistaken.

Just then, her needle hit a particularly sensitive spot, and Nick almost shot out of his chair. "Are you sure you didn't work for Hitler in another life?"

"Tsk-tsk! No pain, no gain," she remarked blithely.

"Easy for you to say! What kind of tattoo are you putting there anyhow? It better not be one of those hokey snakes. Or a skull and crossbones. I want something to impress Paula, not gross her out. How about two linked hearts?"

"Puh-leeze, I'm an artiste. I am creative. I am—"

"—a fraud," he muttered under his breath.

"I heard that, young man," she said. "Watch your mouth, or I won't help you anymore. And I still think you should have let me put the tattoo on your privates. It's the latest thing, you know."

"Get real!"

"Would you consider a genital earring?"

"You're not getting within a mile of these family jewels." He placed both hands protectively over said treasures. "And you'd better hurry up. I only have another ten minutes left on my lunch hour."

Finally, she finished and told him how to care for the tattoo over the next few days. He tried to peer at her creation over his shoulder, but she kept distracting him, blabbing on about how she'd gotten a ticket the day before for failing to procure a business license, and could he fix it for her. He kept telling her he didn't work in that division, but somehow she managed to talk him into seeing what he could do.

After putting his shirt back on and slapping fifty dollars on the table, he asked the question he'd wanted to ask for the past half hour—the real reason he'd stopped by to visit Madame Nadine once again. "So, how do you think I'm doing on this heart craving business?"

Madame Nadine blew a smoke ring the size of an inner tube his way, and, in the midst of his coughing, she said, "You tell me, sonny boy. Has she torn up the divorce papers yet?"

"No," he said on a groan of despair.

"Is she weakening?"

Remembering last night's senior prom fantasy, Nick felt his face grow hot. Since he never blushed, he figured it must be the lack of air-conditioning.

Madame Nadine raised an eyebrow questioningly. When he declined to tell her the intimate details, she smiled knowingly. "Some progress then, huh?"

"A little, but not enough. The bottom line here is that I have less than three days. Any clues on how I can speed this along?"

She looked down at his crotch, then over to her tray of tiny earring loops.

"Forget it!"

He was already headed for the door, ignoring her chuckles, when she added, "I don't suppose you'd like to give your wife a cat? Gargoyle's gettin' bored with me . . . seems to be lookin' for a new home."

"No way! Absolutely not! Never!" He looked back at the feline parked on her lap, a tabby the size of a small automobile, and shivered. It was licking its chops and gazing at him with a condescending I-know-something-you-don't cat grin, probably thinking, "What a chump!"

Nick's upper lip curled with distaste. "I hate cats."

"I know."

"Huh?"

"Maybe you should learn to conquer your fears."

"Maybe you should stick to hair plucking and crystal fish bowls. I will never, *ever* have a cat for a pet."

He turned toward the door again.

"Not even if it could help you get your wife back?"

"Not even if my life depended on it." He slammed the door resoundingly and leaned against the doorframe, wheezing. The mere thought of living with a cat revolted him. He felt like upchucking.

He closed his eyes briefly and fought the picture of a five-year-old boy in the projects. Rats. So many rats! And all those cats chasing them. And his poor baby sister, Lita, in her crib, trapped . . . oh, Lord!

Stiffening with resolve, he forced the bad memories aside. No, he didn't need any damn cat to remind him of all he'd left behind. Not in this lifetime!

When he arrived back at the station house a short time later, he met Skip coming out. Skip stopped dead in his tracks and gaped at him. "What the hell is that giant furball sitting on your front seat?"

"Gargoyle."

"You mean Garfield."

"No, I mean Gargoyle."

"It must weigh fifty pounds. I thought you hated cats."

Nick said a very foul word and stomped past him up the steps, without answering. He was in a cold sweat from having sat next to a cat for the past fifteen minutes. He wanted to go take a shower, brush his teeth, and spray himself with a film of disinfectant.

"Hey, have you given any more thought to that Indian stripper job I mentioned?"

Nick said two foul words and added a hand gesture.

Chapter Six

He'd been schnookered by an expert schnookerer . . .

BY THE TIME Nick quit work that evening, he was in a really bad mood.

His first mission was to unload the cat. So he headed to Paula's.

She declined his gift, graciously but firmly. "Nick, I already have Gonzo. What would I want with a cat?"

In the background, the German shepherd was barking and growling like crazy, straining to leap through the barely opened doorway. Gonzo hated cats almost as much as Nick did.

Paula refused to let Nick come inside her apartment, reminding him that they'd agreed last night to stop seeing each other altogether and accept the fact that they'd be divorced in three more days.

Nick wanted to point out that he'd never agreed to any such thing, but he had more important concerns. *She's not gonna take the damn cat! Oh, Lord! Now what?* Nick's cold sweat turned colder, and a visible shudder passed over his body.

"What am I gonna do with a cat?" he complained. He stood in the hallway, shifting from leg to leg, his arms aching from holding the monster cat that was gaining weight by the second.

"Take it back where you got it. And stop buying things for me without asking. I'm sick of you making decisions for me. If I want a cat, I'll get one myself."

"Talk about ingratitude!"

She glared at him. "And, Nick . . . don't come back tonight. I won't be here." Her lips trembled and her voice cracked. "Last night was an ending. Give up! I don't know how much more I can take."

He gazed at her bleakly.

She peered closer at the cat then. "Nick, that cat's awfully big. Are you sure it's not pregnant?"

"Come again?" He looked at the giant shedding machine in his arms, which was smirking up at him. "It couldn't be. It's a guy cat. Isn't it?" He lifted it up by its front legs and looked where he thought the evidence should be. Nope, no cat penis, as far as he could tell.

His eyes widened with sudden understanding. Then, swearing a blue streak, he spun on his heel and stomped down the hallway.

"Nick, what's wrong? Where are you going?"

"I'm off to kill a fortune teller."

But of course Madame Nadine wasn't at home. He knocked till his knuckles grew raw. He peered, then shouted through the closed windows.

But no answer.

She was probably out cruising the parkway on her broom.

He thought about leaving Gargoyle on the porch, but decided against that when he looked at the busy highway behind him. Even he wasn't into cat roadkill.

That night he discovered two things. He still hated cats. And Gargoyle loved SpaghettiOs and cherry Kool-Aid, the only food he had in the house.

Day Five

Not the roommate he'd been hoping for . . .

The next morning he discovered two more things. Gargoyle had parked herself at the foot of his bed. And she planned a permanent stay, as evidenced by the hissing noise she made every time he tried to pick her up and take her to his car. Scratches up and down his forearms proved the cat had marked his apartment for her new home.

Well, Nick had a few plans of his own. He was going to Pet Control first thing this morning and get a tranquilizer gun. Then he was going to deliver a package—a very large package—to the psychic from hell.

After he showered, he filled the tub with a week's worth of dirty dishes, squirted on a half bottle of dish detergent, and turned on the shower again. It was a trick Skip had taught him.

Then he searched the pile of dirty clothes on the floor of his bedroom for a reasonably clean shirt. He was forced to run a streak of white-out along the inside of the collar. Another dumb-man trick Skip had recommended.

Before he left for work, he wagged his finger in the cat's face, warning, "If you dare to have one single baby while I'm at work, I'm making cat soup. No, cat-and-fortune-teller soup."

Gargoyle, of course, just ignored him, licking her fur with decided indifference.

"And don't breathe on anything while I'm gone. And make sure you confine your cat business to that box of rags in the bathroom. I'll have you know I gave up my favorite ten-year-old Jockey shorts for your crap."

Gargoyle shot him a look down her haughty nose that said clearly, in female cat body language, "You are *so* crude. And dumber than catnip."

At least they had similar tastes in food . . .

NICK ARRIVED home at four, carrying a shopping bag with a gallon of milk and five cans of cat food. For himself, he had a six-pack of beer, ten more cans of SpaghettiOs, and a box of Froot Loops. The cat would have to share the milk.

Pet Control had told him he couldn't tranquilize the cat if it was pregnant. So between assignments that day, he'd driven over to Madame Nadine's, alone. Six times! There was no answer to his repeated pounding on Madame Nadine's door or his shouted threats, although he could swear he saw cigarette smoke through the window.

Before he even unpacked his bags, Nick picked up the phone and dialed Paula's number—for the zillionth time that day. Once again, he got her answering machine and slammed the phone back into the receiver. Paula was avoiding him big time. Apparently, she'd been serious about their not seeing each other again until the divorce hearing.

Well, he would show her he could be just as determined. But first, he had to feed the damn cat, which was rubbing itself against his pant leg and meowing in a disgustingly coaxing fashion. Holding his nose, he opened the can of cat food—"Tuna Milanese"—and dumped the gelatinous mass onto a plate on the floor. *Yech!* Next, he poured a saucer of milk.

Gargoyle lapped up the milk but ignored the cat food disdainfully. Instead, she eyed the SpaghettiOs he was eating cold from the can, washed down with a Bud Light. He tried to ignore her as he put away his purchases, but her eyes followed him accusingly. Finally, he gave up in disgust and dumped the rest of the SpaghettiOs onto another plate and put it on the floor. "I wouldn't eat that tuna, either."

The cat meowed a delicate, "Thank you."

"Don't think this means I like you. Or that you're staying."

"Meow."

"Tomorrow you and I are breaking down Madame Nadine's door."

"Meow."

"I don't suppose you did any laundry today."

Step Two of the Dumb Man's Master Plan . . .

AFTER SHOWERING and gathering together some items Skip had lent him, Nick headed toward Paula's place. He wasn't surprised when she didn't answer the door.

No problem.

After picking the lock, he hurried to shut off the delayed ring of the security alarm, which Paula had turned on, for once. He quickly punched a series of numbers into the keypad, breathing a sigh of relief. What he didn't need was the police showing up.

Then, checking out Paula's answering machine tapes for the past few days, he got a pretty good idea of where she was hiding out. Her parents' beach house at Long Beach Island.

He grinned with satisfaction. Paula's location worked very nicely into the next item on his fantasy agenda. Yes, indeed! Sand . . . lots of sand. He rubbed his hands together with relish.

Paula, baby, this is going to be a night you'll never forget.

Pulling out his wallet, he found the business card he'd been given earlier that day. "Mr. Saleem? Hi, this is Nick DiCello. Yeah, we're still on for tonight, but listen, Omar, there's been a slight change in location." He gave the guy directions to the beach house and told him he'd meet the work crew there in two hours.

"May Allah bless all your plans."

"I sure hope so."

"Do you still want me to contact that traveling circus?"

"Yeah. Sure. And don't forget all the props we discussed. The palm trees, brazier, the cushions—lots of cushions."

"A thousand pardons, my friend, but you've gone over this list with me three times already today."

Nick could hear a calculator clicking in the background.

"You do realize, Mr. DiCello, that this is going to be a *very* expensive evening."

"I expect it to be worth every dollar. And then some." *Even if it sucks up all my savings.*

"Well, 'tis said Allah put woman on earth for a man's pleasure. Are you sure you don't want me to send a belly dancer for entertainment?"

"Nope. I'm planning my own entertainment."

"Welcome to my tent, Desert Flower," said the sheik, or some such hogwash . . .

PAULA HAD BEEN walking the beach for hours. Nightfall approached as the setting sun cast an orange backdrop to the blue ocean, and still she strolled aimlessly, her bare toes skimming the foamy edge of the cool water.

Her family had purchased the cottage on Long Beach Island for a summer home at her birth, nearly thirty years ago. She knew the shoreline like the palm of her hand. And yet it was ever-changing, like her life.

Thoughtfully, she picked up a sea shell, examining its intricate, beautiful whorls, and remembered with a slight smile how she and her young girlfriends used to search fervently for that one shell that would yield a priceless pearl.

And she remembered as a grown woman once reading some philosopher who likened those pearls to temples built by pain around a single grain of sand.

Like Nick's love. So beautiful, but so much pain surrounding it.

She started to throw the shell back into the water, but then whimsically tucked it into the pocket of her shorts.

A heavy cloak of depression weighed her down, as it had all day. She'd escaped Nick physically, but not emotionally. And she doubted she ever would.

She loved the man—totally. But she couldn't live with him.

Thinking about their divorce made her shudder with hurt. And, more important, she knew that she was hurting Nick terribly. But she truly believed he needed the divorce to start healing, as much as she did.

Sometimes, walking away is the greatest expression of love.

Nick just didn't understand—she knew that—but he probably never would. Coming from different backgrounds—she, an only child raised in the sheltered, loving arms of a middle-class suburban family; he, one of five kids barely surviving in a one-bedroom ghetto apartment—they would probably never see things in exactly the same way. That would have been okay. In fact, it had been more than okay at the beginning of their marriage.

But in the last few years, his need to protect her had grown into an obsession. Suffocating her. Changing him. The numerous locks on their doors. A guard dog. A need to know her whereabouts every minute of the day. Attempting to control her activities and her friends. Even her choice of employment.

Worse, he drew more and more into himself, refusing to share his troubles or talk about his work.

A prison. For him, as well as her.

Yes, their marriage would have to end, and she couldn't bear the torture of seeing him again. Each time, the pain tore her apart. Being together made their inevitable parting harder for both of them. Two more days until the hearing. Then their marriage would be over.

With a deep sigh, she turned around and headed back toward the beach house. It was the off-season, so hardly any of the houses were occupied.

Glancing sideways, she saw several trucks parked along the road that ran parallel to the beach—Omar's Special Events Catering, two pickup trucks, and, of all things, a huge animal transport vehicle, with the words CLYDE BEADER TRAVELING CIRCUS stenciled on the side.

She laughed. Someone must be having a party. The residents of this exclusive private beach could afford the most expensive theme parties, and they often tried to outdo themselves with the bizarre.

She turned the bend around a large sand dune that protected against beach erosion and screened their property from the neighbors. Jerking to a quick stop, she stumbled.

At first, she blinked several times, thinking she was seeing a mirage. "Oh, my God!"

A large, low white tent, its fabric billowing in the slight evening breeze, stood on the beach in front of her parents' house. Torches flamed on tall spikes at each of the corners and near an oasis.

An oasis! Her mouth dropped open in amazement. A portable hot tub had been set up on the beach, surrounded by enormous fake palm trees and exotic flowers.

"GR-ONK, GR-ONK!"

Paula jumped at the loud—very loud—nasal call of some animal. Incredibly, a large beast ambled out from behind one of the palm trees.

A camel!

How could that be? A camel on the Jersey shore? Impossible! Local ordinances didn't permit the littlest dogs on a beach these days, let alone a camel. Her brow furrowed with puzzlement.

Then she noticed the black-haired, dark-skinned man sitting cross-legged in front of the open flap of the tent, staring at her somberly like some desert sultan. Dressed in full Arab dress, from long, black robe to matching head cloth, tied in place with a ropelike piece of material, his shoulders were thrown back arrogantly, with all the pride of the most potent Arab sheik.

Nick.

She was going to kill him. She really was.

But before she could scream out her rage or storm up to the stubborn jerk, two large Arab guards grabbed her from behind. They wore similar flowing robes, covered with concealing burnooses. They quickly tied her hands behind her back and wrapped a silk scarf around her mouth, gagging her. One of them picked her up and carried her over to the front of the tent, dropping her to the soft Persian carpet on the sand. She immediately squirmed upright and tried to stand, but one of the brutes shoved her to her knees in front of the sheik.

"Mrffmfh!" She looked back over her shoulder to glare at the two of them, and her eyes almost popped out with disbelief.

Skip winked at her and grinned with wicked appreciation at her situation. Lee Chin was laughing so hard that silent tears ran down his face. Then they both bowed low in dramatic obeisance before the sheik and salaamed, placing their right palms to their foreheads.

"Master Raschid, we bring you the slave girl, Zara. Will you accept her for your harem?"

The sheik—rather, Nick—studied her insolently, as if he wasn't sure. Paula thought about whacking him with a piece of nearby driftwood, but one of the "guards" still held a hand on her shoulder in restraint.

"We shall see," Nick said, rubbing a forefinger thoughtfully over his upper lip, "if she pleases me."

Me please him? Hah! "Mrffmfh!"

She heard Skip and Lee chuckle behind her, but they stopped immediately at Nick's imperious glare. With a curt nod, he dismissed them, stating, with a hand over his heart, "Peace be to you." And she thought she heard him murmur in an aside, "Now, get lost!"

They returned the hand-over-heart gesture. "And peace to you, *master.*"

Master? Hah! "Mrffmfh!"

Skip remarked to Lee as they walked off, "I'd like to be a fly on that camel's butt when Paula gets her hands free."

"I think Nick's goin' stark ravin' bonkers, myself," Lee opined. "No woman's worth makin' a fool of yourself like that."

"Do you think he's makin' a fool of himself? No way! Women eat this romance fantasy stuff up like candy. You really oughtta watch more *The Woman's Edge with Dr. Sheila.*"

"I got better things to do than—"

"Betcha didn't know what some couples do on top of a washing machine."

"Huh?"

Skip gave a short, graphic account of laundry room sexual activity, most of it revolving around vibrating washing machines.

Impressed, Lee asked, "And you learned that from Dr. Sheila? Wow!"

Paula's face flamed with embarrassment. Good Lord! By tomorrow morning, everyone in New Jersey was going to know about this latest stunt of Nick's. And it would be linked right up there with vibrating washing machines.

She gritted her teeth, closed her eyes, and counted to ten for patience. Finally, she opened her eyes and looked at Nick.

He still sat cross-legged in front of her with his arms folded across his chest. He stared at her with blatant sexual interest, not even trying to hide his intentions.

"Mrffmfh!"

"Would you like me to remove the gag, Zara?" he asked in a soft voice.

She nodded vigorously.

"Do you promise not to scream?"

"Mrffmfh!" Her eyes flashed sparks of defiance. Oh, she

intended to scream all right. And slap some sense into his silly head.

He laughed, a low, throaty sound. "Ah, then, we cannot allow that. It appears you need to understand your role, my dear. I will, of course, enjoy teaching you."

Her eyebrows shot up at that.

And little tingles of unwanted pleasure rippled across Paula's skin at the erotic promise in his voice.

A slow, knowing grin tugged at Nick's beautiful lips. "I wonder what kind of pupil you will be, Zara."

I wonder, too. Oh, Lord!

"Will you be defiant and resist me, like a proud desert princess? Or will you be compliant and seductive, like an experienced *houri*?"

Every nerve ending in her body leaped to attention at those vivid mind pictures.

He stood and walked behind her, so close that she could feel the soft caress of his robe against her bare leg, the whisper of his breath against her hair. Abruptly, before she could react, he lifted her by both upper arms and propelled her inside the tent, closing the flap behind him.

And the fantasy began.

Chapter Seven

On a scale of one to ten, this sexual fantasy was a twenty . . .

PAULA FELT AS if she had fallen into a black hole and emerged on the other side of the world. It was *Arabian Nights* and a torrid Bertrice Small novel all wrapped up in one.

By the flickering light of candles and tall flame-lit torches, she saw jewel-toned Persian carpets, topped with dozens of satin pillows. Wine cooled in an ice-filled bucket, and succulent Middle Eastern foods warmed over a brazier. Exotic music came from somewhere—a mournful twang reminiscent of hot Sahara nights and dark-skinned Bedouin lovers.

Paula fought the seductive pull of the erotic fantasy Nick was creating for her. She didn't understand why he did it, but she couldn't deny the heightening of her senses—or the lowering of her resistance. She closed her eyes, fighting for control, and groaned behind her gag.

"Did you say something, Zara?"

Nick had come up behind her, silent as a desert bandit, and placed a sharp blade near her throat. She glanced back over her shoulder at him. A shiver ran through her, but not of fear. Nick wouldn't hurt her.

Before she realized what he intended, he cut her oversized T-shirt from the neck band to the end of the short sleeves on both sides. Despite her hands being still bound behind her back, he was able to pull the shirt down till it fell to the ground, exposing her bare breasts. They peaked immediately into telling points of aching arousal. She wore only shorts now, but those, and her panties, soon joined her shirt on the ground.

And she stood before him, naked and vulnerable, like the

slave captive he had deemed her.

He circled her in a predatory fashion, examining her body from all angles, as if determining her worth. Nick had always been a good actor. That was why he often got assigned to drug busts or gigs where he had to play a role. He was using all those talents now. If Paula hadn't known him before, she would swear he really was a ruthless sheik who'd captured an unwilling slave girl . . . on a New Jersey beach.

She giggled, low in her throat.

"You find humor in your captivity, do you, Zara?" he asked in a velvety voice, and trailed the dull side of his knife downward, flicking the nipples of both breasts lightly.

She inhaled sharply at the intense pleasure.

He smiled. "I'm going to remove your gag now, Zara, and you are not to speak unless I give you permission. I am the master. You are my slave. Do you understand?"

At first, she remained obstinate. Then she nodded her head. Despite herself, she was curious as to just how far he would go with this charade.

The minute the silk scarf fell away from her mouth, she charged, "Nick, you can't do this."

"Oh, can't I?" he said. "Did I not tell you to remain silent? I am Raschid. It is the only name I will answer to. Or master."

She made an "in your dreams" snort of disgust.

He raised an eyebrow at her in challenge and continued, "And you are Zara . . . my love slave."

Love slave? Oh, my.

"What is this, some kind of middle-aged crazy thing?"

"Middle-aged?" he sputtered indignantly. "I'm only thirty-five. And you're doing a hell of a lot more drooling than I am."

"Pre-middle-aged then. Or post-raging-stud-dom. All I know is, you're acting crazy lately."

"Stud-dom?" He grinned, honing in on that one word. "You think I'm still a stud?"

"Still?" She made another snort of disgust.

"Now, now, sarcasm does not befit a harem girl." He

winked and held out a bundle of sheer fabric. "When I release your hands, *slave*, you will put this on," he ordered.

Paula looked down in puzzlement as he shook the fabric out, causing all the tiny bells sewn along its edges to tinkle delightfully. She couldn't help but smile . . . until she realized what he held. A harem girl's outfit—like a belly dancer's—little more than transparent scarves that would reveal more than they would hide. Oh, this was outrageous! And, worst of all, it probably belonged to one of the strippers at Skip's nightclub.

"No."

"No?

"You can't make me."

"Think again, *slave*."

"Hah!" *I'd like to know how—*

"I could tie you to a tent pole and caress you till your tongue curls."

"Hah!" *He wouldn't dare. Would he?*

"I could lay you on those pillows and slather you with honey and lick you from your toenails to your eyebrows."

"Hah!" *Oh, he is good.*

"I could give you a new lesson in aural sex, talking—just talking—for hours about the things I fantasize about doing to you, until you come, and come, and come."

"Hah!" *Stop panting, Paula, or he'll know you're interested.*

"I could touch myself the way I would like you to touch me and force you to watch."

Oh, my God!

"I could stick dates in—"

"Stop!" she choked out. "Give me the damn bimbo clothes."

He laughed smoothly and untied the scarf binding her wrists behind her back, then handed her the sheer garment. Turning away, he poured two glasses of wine while she dressed, which didn't take long, considering the small amount of fabric.

The top portion was a red chiffon, bolero-style vest, with no buttons or clasps, ending just under her breasts. The loose pantaloons, also of red chiffon, hung low on her hips, exposing her navel. Tiny bells lined all the gold twining edges of both the top and bottom garments.

Paula felt more exposed than if she were naked.

And she felt incredibly sexy. Especially with Nick still being fully clothed.

She got grim satisfaction when he turned, and his jaw dropped with surprise. He almost spilled the glass of wine he was about to hand her.

"Hot damn!" he murmured under his breath.

She walked closer to him, jingling like a Christmas sleigh—*just call me Tinkerbell*—and reached for the glass of wine.

"Well?" she asked, wanting to reverse the tables on him, to take over the reins in this power play. She experienced an odd thrill in knowing she could turn him on so easily. She felt an even greater thrill wondering how it would feel to play out this tantalizing drama. "Does this fulfill your fantasy?"

A grin teased at his lips. "Allah be praised. You are every man's dream. But this is to be your fantasy, Zara. For your pleasure, if Allah wills."

Suddenly, Paula was frightened of this game and how easily she had fallen, once again, under Nick's spell. They shouldn't be talking, let alone having sex, with their divorce a few days off. Not only was Nick going off the deep end, but now she was about to take the leap, too. "All right, Nick. You've had your big joke. Now, tell me what this is all about."

"Not Nick. Raschid," he corrected. "And you need not understand the fantasy. Do not fight the fates Allah has foretold."

She put both hands on her hips, stamping her foot.

His eyes flashed blue fire, darkening with passion, as they riveted on her chest.

She looked down and groaned. Her posture had caused the vest to part, exposing a good portion of her breasts. She jerked the sides together and scowled at him.

He smiled, a dazzling display of white teeth and pure Nick charm. She melted. She couldn't stay mad at him when he smiled at her like that. She never could.

That is, until he spoke his next words.

"You will feed me now, *slave*."

"I beg your pardon," she said with disbelief.

He dropped down languidly to a nest of cushions, sipping at his wine, and pointed to the brazier. "A good slave feeds her master . . . with her fingers."

Paula took a long drink of her wine to cool her consternation—and ardor—but it had the opposite effect. The potent beverage rushed to all the nerve centers in her body, heightening their sensitivity. Even the air teased her skin, which had become one large canvas of unending erogenous zones.

"This is the twenty-first century, babe—I mean, Raschid," she snapped, fighting the whirl of her dizzying emotions, "and women don't *serve* men."

Paula knew she'd made a mistake almost immediately. She downed the rest of her glass of wine in a big gulp as Nick rose in one fluid motion and pushed her gently to the cushions. "Of course, you are right, Zara. I will serve you."

And he did.

Half reclining on the cushions, sipping at the second glass of wine Nick handed her, Paula had trouble concentrating. Perhaps it was the effects of the alcohol. More likely, it was the enticing feel of Nick's fingers against her lips, feeding her rice with slivers of succulent lamb, bite-sized pieces of pita bread dripping with honey, marinated olives, and sweet dates.

Along the way, somehow, she'd begun to feed him as well. He lay on his side, leaning on one elbow, with a tray of food between them. His expression was hungry and lustful, and she thrilled at the knowledge that food was only the appetizer in this delicious foreplay.

When she placed a pomegranate seed inside his mouth, he held her wrist in place and sucked the pulp surrounding the kernel till she finally removed it from his mouth. Over and over, she repeated the procedure, fascinated by the play of light and shadow on his flexing cheeks, increasingly excited by the abrasion of his tongue on her thumb and forefinger.

"I would like to do the same with your nipples," he said

huskily, holding her eyes.

And when she put the next seed in his mouth, she felt each pull in her breasts.

"Do you feel it, Zara?"

She couldn't answer, but he knew. He knew.

"Bare your breasts for me, slave."

She had probably had too much to drink. That could be the only explanation for her even considering doing as he asked. Sitting up, she watched as he removed the tray between them. Then, slowly, she drew her bolero apart and over her shoulders.

Nick made a low growl of approval.

She lay back down, feeling as seductive as the Bedouin princess she pretended to be. Nick gazed at her like a thirsty man who just arrived at a sand-locked oasis, about to be offered his first cup of water. And Paula realized that the last thing in the world she wanted was to make him suffer.

"Arch your back, Zara, like a cat. Purr for your master. Can you purr?"

She could. And she did.

The Middle Eastern music thrummed around them, exotic and sexually compelling.

All of Paula's blood seemed to center and pump rhythmically in the fullness of her breasts, which she offered to him wantonly. Leaning back on both elbows, she threw her head back with shameless abandon, concentrating all her attention on the pebble-hard tips.

She was no longer Paula. She was a desert princess, and Nick was her sheik, the answer to her most intimate dreams.

Tossing aside his headdress, he rose to his knees at her side, his adoring eyes raking her body.

With his hands at his sides, he bent forward, and his hot breath fanned her breast as he whispered, "You are my beloved, and I am your slave."

Paula keened aloud then with the intensity of her need and arched higher, forcing her nipple against his lips. He chuckled softly with delight.

"No, I am the slave. I must be a slave to bend to your will so easily," she whispered.

When he kissed the taut buds, then drew on them gently and laved them with his tongue, she began to whimper and tried to pull away. Wave after wave of pleasure mingled with pain washed over her, and Nick put one arm under her back to hold her in the arched position. He would not let her escape now.

For long minutes he played the two hardened "seeds," overt marks of her overwhelming arousal. Alternately, he used his lips and tongue and teeth to nip and caress, suck and blow, flick and press.

Her thighs grew rigid as she strained, fighting against the onslaught of her approaching climax. "Stop. It's too much. Please. Oh. Please."

But he would not comply. "Yield, Zara," he coaxed her in a thickened voice. "Surrender to me."

Then, suddenly, he stopped and stood, pulling her to her feet. The tiny bells on her trousers jingled.

Blinking, barely able to focus through the haze of her inflamed senses, Paula watched as Nick drew away from her and leaned against a tent pole, folding his arms casually over his chest. But there was nothing casual about his pale eyes, glistening like beautiful pools of blue passion, or his full lips, parted sensually.

She couldn't believe he was going to just stop. How could he? Nick had never been so cruel.

"Will you dance for me now, Zara?" he asked in a low, erotic growl.

"I don't know how," she protested weakly, but already her hips swayed seductively to the rhythm of the Arab music. The bells jingled softly as she moved.

She found she *could* dance. For Nick.

Raising her hands to the nape of her neck, she lifted her hair. She looked back at him over her shoulder and saw that he'd shifted back into his role-playing. He watched her intently, his face an expressionless mask, like some caliph viewing a harem girl. And that bothered her. A lot. Hah! She'd show him.

Paula turned and lifted her own breasts. *Oh, Lord, did I really do that?*

A muscle twitched near his lips.

Good! She rolled her shoulders. Slowly.

His lips parted.

So, the caliph isn't a eunuch, after all? She picked up a set of finger cymbals and clicked them in tune with the music.

He gasped softly.

So, he'd like to lock her in a harem, would he? Well, maybe she was more woman than he could handle. She undulated her hips.

He began to smile.

All the time, she held Nick's eyes.

He began to disrobe, showing her how very much he wanted her.

And Paula forgot where the game ended and reality began. The molten heat that had been centered in her breasts gushed in a torrent to all the extremities of her body and pooled in a simmering mass between her legs. She felt hot, and desirable, and all woman. She would do anything for Nick. Anything.

"And does this slave please her master, Raschid?" she whispered, coming up close to Nick, circling him, teasing him with swaying hips, trailing fingertips across his wide shoulders.

When he reached for her, she slipped away, laughing gaily. The second time she approached, he grabbed her by the waist and pulled her hard against his body, chortling triumphantly. Pressing his lips to the wildly beating pulse in her neck, he rasped, "This slave pleases her master mightily." And he took her hand, curling her palm around his "might."

Desire licked like hot flames through Nick's body as his wide palms swept over his wife's bare back. He nuzzled the shadowy hollow of her neck and savored the familiar scent of her lemony cologne.

This was Paula, the woman he loved more than life. And this was Zara, the alluring *houri,* who could enchant a Bedouin raider. They were one and the same.

Slipping his hands into the back waistband of her trousers, he cupped her buttocks and pulled her hard against his erection, lifting her feet off the carpet. "I want you," he rasped.

She undulated her hips against him. "I know." Her eyes sparkled teasingly.

He laughed. "You take to your role very well, slave. I wonder, will you be able to hold my *attention* all through the night?"

"Hah!" she said, ducking under his arm and stepping out of her trousers to stand before him, proud and unashamed of her nudity. "I wonder if you will be able to *hold* your attention all through the night."

Then she amazed him by walking to the bed of cushions and lying down on her back. She raised her hands above her head and parted her legs slightly, posing for him with an abandon he would have never thought possible for his Paula. "I yield to you, my master. You may have your will with me now. Your wish is my command."

Nick dropped to his knees. Then, nudging her legs farther apart, he moved on top of her. Braced on his elbows, he slanted his lips over hers and began to enter her body, whispering, "My wish is to make love to my wife. My wish is that you surrender to me . . . everything."

He saw the brief flicker of fear in her eyes, felt the tightening of her arm and thigh muscles. "No, no, darling, don't be afraid. All I ask is your complete trust." He knew she wondered if she would be surrendering to more than one night's madness. But, gradually, she relaxed and gave herself up to him.

Nick controlled the pace of their lovemaking then. He slowed his thrusts, even as she urged him with throaty cries to end her torture. When her body began to convulse around him, he held himself rigid until her orgasm stopped. Then he began the rhythm again.

"I'm dying," she moaned as she writhed from side to side.

"Then we are dying together." Desperate and obsessed, Nick fought to make this night last forever. He had to convince Paula, if only with his lovemaking, that they belonged together.

His caresses became frantic. He lay beside her, over her, under her. Touching and exploring every inch of her body.

Memorizing. Her heat and the intensity of her orgasms and regenerating arousals enveloped him and spurred him toward his own climax. Relentlessly, he resisted the release.

But the force of his need eventually overpowered him.

Sucking in deep, soul-drenching draughts of air, he hurtled toward a mind-blowing pinnacle. Bracing himself on straightened arms, he threw his head back, feeling the cords in his neck stand out, and cried out triumphantly as he exploded inside her body's convulsing folds.

He must have passed out for a few moments, or slept, from the intensity of his climax. When his brain emerged from its fuzzy state of confused satiety, he felt Paula's hands caressing his shoulders and back, crooning soft words of pleasure and encouragement . . . love words. Even though he lay heavily on her, she didn't protest. Tears burned his eyes, and he blinked them back. He didn't think he could love his wife more than he did at that moment.

He raised his head. "Paula, honey, I love you so much."

"I know, Nick. I know. I love you, too." She brushed a wisp of hair off his brow, sweaty from their exertions. And the gesture displayed as much caring as the most intimate caress.

Hope blossomed like a desert flower in his heart. "Paula, does this mean that—"

"Shhh, not now. No talking," she said. "If we talk, I'll have to think. And I don't want to think. Just feel."

"Well, then, my desert flower, perhaps I can help you feel some more," he said, rolling to his side and propping himself on one elbow, gazing down at her. Lightly, he ran a forefinger from the curve of her neck, down over the peak of one breast, over her belly button, to the damp curls of her womanhood.

She sighed. "I don't think I'm capable of any more feeling."

He quirked an eyebrow. "Ah, that sounds like a challenge to me. We Bedouin warriors have a reputation to uphold."

She giggled.

"You doubt me, wench? Hmmm. Well, since we have no female harem girls here to serve you, I will have to act as your handmaiden. Turn over on your stomach, Zara. I will minister to your weak body . . . bring it back to life."

He stood and picked up the beaker that was warming on the far side of the brazier.

"What's that?" she asked suspiciously.

"Warm oil to massage your muscles, which are sadly out of shape from lack of use."

"So you think I'm out of shape, do you?" She stretched lazily, and he felt a part of his body stretch, too.

"No, not you, Zara. Just certain muscles." He jiggled his eyebrows as he spoke. "Lie on your stomach, slave, and stop asking questions," he ordered in a mock stern voice.

Surprisingly, she did as he demanded. *Hey, maybe that's where I went wrong. I didn't do enough ordering.*

"GR-ONK! GR-ONK!"

Oh, no!

"What was that?" Paula asked, her head jerking up with alarm.

"Just the camel," Nick said, setting the beaker on the ground.

"Camel! I thought I saw a camel out there. Nick, you're going to get in big, big trouble bringing a camel onto the beach."

"I am Raschid, and Raschid can do anything in his kingdom."

"And Long Beach Island is your kingdom?"

"You betcha, baby. Besides, Raschid knows the local sheriff who owes him many drachmas for a favor I granted him."

"*Hmpfh!* That probably means you squelched a ticket."

Under his breath, he muttered something about a poker game.

"Hey, where are you going? I thought you were going to give me a hot oil massage."

He reached down and slapped her playfully on the tush. "Do not be so anxious, Zara. We have all night. Right now, I am off to feed yon camel."

She grinned. "And what do yon camels eat, oh great desert warrior?"

"Damned if I know," he said with a shrug as he stepped

through the tent flap, bare-assed naked, uncaring if any of the neighbors could see him.

This night was turning out better than he'd ever expected. Even the huge piles of camel dung that he almost stepped in didn't dampen his enthusiasm. Hell, Paula's mother prided herself on her prize dahlias. Surely, camel dung was no different than cow manure, and farmers used that for fertilizer all the time.

After tending to the camel, he returned to the tent, where he massaged the scented oil into Paula's body, and she reciprocated, followed by their making slow, slow love. They laughed softly at the slickness of their bodies, sighing their pleasure at the exquisitely drawn-out foreplay, crying exultantly in unison at the climax.

Then they washed each other's bodies in the jacuzzi oasis and made love again. When he carried her back into the tent, they drank the sweet Arabic tea, pronounced *shay-hee,* from glasses with peanuts at the bottom. He tried to talk Paula into trying the fermented goat's milk, served at room temperature, but she turned up her nose at the strong, unpleasant odor.

"Nick, what in heaven's name is that on your shoulder?"

He grimaced. "A tattoo."

"You got a tattoo? I can't believe it. It's amazing that I didn't notice it before."

"I just got it yesterday," he admitted, "and I suspect you were too occupied to see it last night." He flashed her a knowing, very satisfied look.

She blushed in remembrance. "But why would you get a tattoo?"

"For you," he stated flatly.

She frowned in puzzlement.

"You see, there was this fortune-teller, and I was asking for advice, and she said women like these things, but I didn't know she was gonna put a sunflower on my back. I thought it was gonna be something sexy like—hell, I don't know what I expected." He took a deep breath after his long-winded explanation.

A frown of confusion still furrowed her brow.

He pinched her bottom playfully. "Hey, you're lucky I didn't do what she really wanted . . . pierce my genitals and hang an earring there." He pointed downward.

"Oh, you!" Paula said finally. "I should have known you were just kidding."

If you only knew, babe!

Smiling, they fell asleep in each other's arms, sated and happy.

Day Six
Another speed bump on the Clueless Highway . . .

Morning light already filtered into the tent when Nick awakened to the rustling of fabric. He rolled over lazily and opened his eyes halfway. Paula was dressing as best she could in the revealing harem costume. He decided then and there that he wouldn't return the outfit to Skip's boss. Instead, he'd buy it for Paula, a memento of this fantasy interlude. Maybe they'd take it out every year on this date, an anniversary of sorts.

"Where are you going, honey?" He stretched, and his knee and elbow joints creaked. He was getting too old for this stuff. *Yeah, right.*

She looked down at him lovingly and shook her head helplessly. "You are the only man I know who wakes up in a good mood. I love that about you. Did I ever tell you that before?"

"You wake up with that many men, huh?"

"You know darn well you're the only one, you brute. And it's not fair that you can look so sexy first thing in the morning."

Damn, I'm good. "I look sexy? Hmmm. Maybe you'd better come back to bed, sweetheart, and show me just how sexy."

She pretended horror. "Not again, Nick. I can barely walk."

He grinned at her and sat up. "I like that. Come here, you. I want to kiss you good morning." He held out his arms.

She hesitated, then walked over and sat next to him.

"I love you, Paula," he said solemnly as he kissed her lightly.

She grazed her knuckles over his bristly jaw and whispered, "And I love you, Nick. I never stopped."

"We're going to work this out, Paula. Aren't we?"

"I think so . . . I hope so, Nick. It seems like an impossible task, but every time I'm with you, well, it just keeps getting better and better. I'm finding it awfully hard to imagine living without you."

Thank you, God! And God bless Madame Nadine. I think I'll buy her a new crystal ball. Maybe even a new dress. Heck, maybe she'd like a truckload of camel dung for her sunflowers.

Chuckling softly at his whimsical thoughts, he kissed her gently and tried to pull her down to the cushions again. But she pushed his chest playfully and stood up, adjusting her clothes.

"Sorry, Charlie, but I have an appointment in Newark in three hours."

He lay back with his hands folded behind his neck, watching her try to finger comb her sex-tangled hair. If she could only see the brush burns on her face and neck, her kiss-bruised lips, and the languid passion still evident in her limpid eyes, she wouldn't show herself in public today. Ah, well, he kind of liked the marks of his lovemaking being displayed to the outside world. She belonged to him, and he wanted everyone to know.

"What kind of appointment did you say you have?"

"A job interview . . . at the Patterson projects. I've had three other interviews these past few weeks, but this is the one I really want. I'd be working directly with the kids as a youth activity coordinator, and—what's wrong? Why are you looking at me like that?"

He stood up and hunched over at the waist, inhaling and exhaling deeply, fighting for breath. *Oh, Lord, no! Not now! Just when things are starting to go right again.*

"Nick—Nick, what's wrong?"

"Cancel the interview," he said peremptorily. "Don't go."

"Why not?"

"Because I don't want you to. Can't that be reason enough?"

A cloud of doubt, then gradual comprehension, began to transform the softness of her face, turning it cold. "Already . . . *already*, it's starting again, isn't it, Nick?" Her voice cracked with painful regret.

"Paula, please try to understand. You can't work in the Patterson projects. It's just too dangerous. I'm willing to agree to your being a social worker, even let you work with the city kids. But from a safe point. An office in some government building, maybe. Just not Patterson."

"You're willing to *agree*?" she snapped, anger turning her voice shrill. "How dare you suggest I need your permission to do anything, you jerk?"

"Paula, just try to understand my viewpoint. I have my . . . reasons." He gulped hard, clenching his fists against the tide of despair threatening to crush him.

"Why don't you explain those reasons to me, Nick? For once, be honest. Tell me what frightens you so much. Tell me what it is you have buried so deep inside, that's so painful you can't talk about it, even to me."

He tried to speak, but the words wouldn't come. Bleakly, he admitted, "I can't. Not now. Maybe someday."

"No!" she cried, tears welling in her eyes and streaming down her face. "Someday is never going to come for us. *Never.* I was a fool to think you were changing. A fool." She began to weep and turned away from him.

"I can change, Paula. I am changing. Just give me a little more time. A chance to—"

"No!" she repeated on a sob, shoving away the hand he extended imploringly to her. "I have an appointment that I'm not going to miss. And I'm going to accept the job if it's offered."

"That's what you think," he said coldly. "Is your appointment with Lottie Chancellor, the social service director?"

She turned abruptly with surprise. "Yes. Do you know her?"

He nodded. "I'll call Lottie. I'll tell her not to give you the job."

"You wouldn't!" she gasped, her eyes swimming with tears of hurt.

"You bet your sweet ass I would. I'd do anything to keep you safe. Anything." *Even if it means losing you in the process.*

"You are a bastard. And I never want to see you again after our divorce hearing tomorrow." Her face flushed with anger as she spat out the words.

He flinched.

Without waiting for a response, she flipped open the flap on the tent and stormed out.

Nick gazed dejectedly through the opening toward the ocean. Last night, he'd had his dreams back, within his grasp, and they'd slipped away once again, just like the sand along the shore. It was hopeless. Hopeless.

A second later, Paula rushed back through the doorway, blushing hotly.

His hopes soared.

"Your camel got loose."

His hopes plummeted.

"There are about two dozen kids on the beach chasing that blasted camel of yours in the surf."

She hadn't come back for him.

"And a man named Omar said to ask if you want to keep the tent for another day. Also," she added, looking down at her flimsy outfit, "he had the nerve to offer me a job as a belly dancer."

Nick started to laugh then, deep belly laughs. Despite the sadness of his situation, despite their impending divorce, despite all that he loved and seemed to be losing, he couldn't help himself.

Paula threw her chin up haughtily and wrapped herself in a soft Persian throw rug, walking out again.

But still he laughed and laughed until tears rolled down his cheeks, and he forgot whether he was laughing or crying.

Chapter Eight

Ah! Finally, she was beginning to understand . . .

PAULA'S INTERVIEW was not going well.

First, she'd arrived fifteen minutes late for her appointment with Lottie Chancellor, the head social worker of the Patterson projects, a huge complex of low-income housing.

It had taken her almost an hour to mask the marks of Nick's lovemaking—whisker-burned face and neck, kiss-swollen lips, and hair so tangled she finally just skinned it back into a ponytail. Paula still couldn't believe that whole Arabian Nights scenario Nick had pulled off, or that she'd willingly participated. *Oh, Lord, the things I did! The things he did!*

Then she'd been unable to find a parking place within a block of the project office. Nick would have a heart attack if he could see the side street where she'd eventually left the little VW convertible.

To top it all off, Mrs. Chancellor—she'd emphasized to Paula from the start that she was *Mrs.,* not *Ms.*—kept asking her skeptical questions about her motives in seeking an inner city job. "Mrs. DiCello, you have a good teaching position, an important job, molding young minds. I just can't see why you'd want to work here in the projects."

The tall, bone-thin black woman, with tight, steel-gray curls capping the sharp planes of her face, closed Paula's folder on the desk. Her discerning brown eyes probed Paula intently, as if looking for hidden secrets.

Paula squirmed in her seat, her eyes darting nervously about the shabby, but clean, office. Searching for words, she tried to explain. "I enjoy teaching, but it was never what I really wanted. The biggest problems the nine-year-old kids in my class have are whether their parents will buy them a five-hundred-dollar mountain bike or—"

Mrs. Chancellor gave a short hoot of laughter. "And the nine-year-olds in this neighborhood are figuring out how to steal them."

"—or where they'll go on vacation this summer, the shore or the mountains."

Mrs. Chancellor's face revealed infinite sadness. "Most of my kids will never have a vacation. They either die young or never leave the ghetto."

Paula knew that. Surely, Mrs. Chancellor didn't think she was an insensitive do-gooder with no understanding of the life-and-death struggle urban children faced every day. That was one of the reasons she yearned to help.

Raising her chin stubbornly, she continued to explain herself. "I always intended to go to graduate school right after college, but then . . . well, I got married . . ." *Oh, Lord! When I met Nick, it was like being hit with a Mack truck of sexual attraction. Those were the days! Nick couldn't keep his hands off me. Heck, I couldn't keep my hands off him. School was the last thing I was thinking about then.*

She gulped and went on. "My plans were put aside for a few years. I worked and went to school at night." She held the social worker's eyes with a level stare. "This is my dream, Mrs. Chancellor. I want to *really* make a difference in young people's lives. Children in desperate need."

"It's not safe here for a woman like you," she said flatly.

Like me? Paula bristled. "If I were black, would it be any safer?"

"No."

Paula tossed her hair back over her shoulder, forgetting it was still in a ponytail. "Because I'm a woman?"

Mrs. Chancellor made a rude snorting sound. "I have just as many women as men on my staff. In fact, sometimes women do a better job reaching these children."

"My age? I am twenty-nine, you know."

She shook her head.

"Then what?"

"Your background. Girl, you have no idea what it's like to grow up in a project. To see death on a daily basis. To hunger for a better life and know it's hopeless."

"I can learn," she protested. "And I refuse to accept that it's hopeless."

"Perhaps." Mrs. Chancellor smiled at her vehemence and tapped her pencil thoughtfully on the desk. "Nick would never forgive me if I hired you."

Paula gasped. So that was the reason for Mrs. Chancellor's attitude. "Nick called you?" she asked incredulously.

"Oh, yes, Nick called. Threatened to have me arrested for breaking some law or other. Challenged my morals for even considering your application." Mrs. Chancellor chuckled. "Said he'd stop volunteering for the youth basketball program."

"Nick threatened you? Oh, this is too much! How dare he?"

Mrs. Chancellor waved Paula's indignation aside. "I've known that husband of yours since he was five years old. He doesn't scare me one bit."

Paula thought of something else. "Nick plays basketball with the kids? How long has he been doing that?"

"Two years."

Two years? Before she'd left him. How was it possible that she'd never known? So, all those nights she'd thought he was playing one-on-one at the gym with Skip, he'd actually been down here in the ghetto. Why wouldn't he talk about such an admirable activity?

The answer came to her immediately. He knew she'd want to come along to the projects, and he'd spent years trying to prevent her from doing just that.

"Mrs. Chancellor, Nick and I are getting a divorce. He had no right to call you or—"

"He's worried about you. Don't blame him for caring about your welfare," Mrs. Chancellor chastised her sternly. "Ninety percent of the women in this project have no husbands. What they wouldn't give to have a man—anyone, for that matter—who wanted to protect them! So don't knock the protective instincts of a good man to me, girl."

Paula stiffened. "But Nick goes too far. He—never mind, I didn't come here to discuss my personal problems." She picked up her purse from the floor and stood. "I can see now that this interview was doomed from the beginning. You're never going to hire me with Nick breathing over your shoulder."

"Now, I never said that," Mrs. Chancellor interjected quickly with a sly smile. She pulled a set of keys out of her drawer and stood, towering over Paula. "C'mon, I want to show you something." Without waiting for Paula's agreement, she led her through the door of her office, making sure to lock the three dead bolts. Then she walked briskly down a corridor to the stairway, bypassing the elevator. "Half the time the elevators don't work," she explained, "and the smell inside their close confines is enough to gag a maggot."

The smells were pretty bad in the halls, too, Paula thought, recognizing spaghetti sauce and urine and God only knew what other odors. Graffiti marked the walls, and the sounds of crying children and arguing adults echoed through the thin walls of the units.

She felt like crying.

Hurrying to catch up, she followed the energetic woman up one flight of stairs after another, till they got to the fourth floor.

"This apartment is empty right now," Mrs. Chancellor told her as she inserted a key in the door and entered, motioning for Paula to follow.

Paula looked around at the small combination living room and kitchen. The two windows overlooked the dumpsters on one side and the brick walls of the next building on the other. Sun would rarely brighten these drab rooms.

In the single bedroom, two double beds took up almost the entire space except for a dresser with a cracked mirror. The grimy bathroom had only a sink, a toilet, and a tub with no showerhead.

Coming back to Mrs. Chancellor, Paula raised an eyebrow questioningly, unsure what her prospective employer wanted her to see.

"This is the apartment where Nick grew up with his mother

and four brothers and sisters."

Paula clasped a hand to her heart, and tears welled in her eyes. *Oh, no! Oh, God, no! Such a dismal place!*

"Actually, they weren't as crowded as most families here," Mrs. Chancellor went on. "You know, of course, about Lita?"

Paula nodded. Nick had told her his little sister had died when she was a baby.

"Lita passed on when Nick was only five years old. That's why the authorities called me in. Too bad the little one had to die to bring about any change here." She shook her head woefully in remembrance.

The fine hairs stood out on Paula's neck. She knew the little girl had died, but apparently Nick had left out a few facts. "How did her death bring you here?"

Mrs. Chancellor looked surprised at Paula's question. "You don't know how Lita died?"

Paula hesitated, not sure she wanted to know.

"Rat bites," Mrs. Chancellor informed her bluntly.

Paula exhaled loudly with dismay and sank down to the sofa, realizing immediately that it had a broken spring, and moved to the other side. "Tell me."

"The old superintendent—Wilson—was skimming money out of the projects for years. One of the areas he stole from was pest control. His idea of rat eradication was to bring in cats, dozens of the rat catchers, which, of course, weren't sufficient to curb the rodent population."

Cats? So, that's why Nick hates cats. They remind him of the projects. And rats. She laced her fingers together in her lap to stop their trembling.

"Lita was only one year old, sleeping in her crib. Her mother was out somewhere. Drinking, no doubt. And Nick was in charge of the younger children."

Oh, poor Nick! And only five years old.

Even the hardened Mrs. Chancellor seemed shaken then as she recalled the past. "That summer was especially bad here in the projects. Unrelenting heat. A sanitation strike. And rats." She sighed deeply. "The bottom line is that Lita was bitten repeatedly by rats. Nick didn't understand the seriousness; he was only a kid. And his mother was negligence personified."

"No!" Paula resisted what she suspected was coming next.

"Yes. A rampant infection set in, which wasn't treated for days. Lita died within a week of blood poisoning."

Paula gagged and rushed for the bathroom. When she emerged a short time later, Mrs. Chancellor appeared apologetic. "I shouldn't have told you all that."

"Yes, you should have. Actually, Nick should have told me himself, but—"

Mrs. Chancellor patted her shoulder. "You have to understand the shame, my dear."

"Shame? Why should he feel ashamed? It wasn't his fault."

"I know, I know. But he's a proud young man. The last thing he would want is pity."

Yes, Nick was proud. And stubborn.

"And he felt guilty."

"Guilty?"

"Of course. He'd failed to protect the ones he loved."

Understanding rushed over Paula in a torrent. Now—now when it was too late—she'd been given a reason for Nick's overprotectiveness. A clue to his obsessive behavior. He'd never lied to her about his past, but, oh, he'd omitted so much.

"What about his brothers and sisters?"

"Teresa died of a drug overdose when she was thirteen. Anthony was killed in a gang fight. And Frankie is in prison for grand larceny."

"Nick has a brother who's alive?" Paula didn't know if she could take any more shocks like this today.

Mrs. Chancellor nodded slowly. "You really should talk to your husband."

"No, Nick really should talk to me." *And he would. Oh, yes, he definitely would.*

After that, Mrs. Chancellor showed her around the rest of the projects, including the youth activity rooms where Paula would work if she was hired. Her heart wept as she pictured a young Nick in this setting, scrambling about the makeshift gym after a volleyball game, playing checkers with one of the counselors, fighting off the encroaching decay and evil that hovered outside—and within.

Mrs. Chancellor finally told Paula, "We have a desperate need for help here, Mrs. DiCello. If you want the job, it's yours. But think about it for a few days. Talk to Nick—now, now, don't get your hackles up—he's in a position to give you good advice. Listen to what he has to say. Then call me."

As Paula walked toward her car, she pondered all she'd seen that morning. She put her fingertips to her lips, still bruised from Nick's many kisses. Her body, as well as her emotions, had been battered the past week. The upcoming divorce. Her job search. Nick's refusal to accept the end of their marriage. His persistent, endearing efforts to woo her back.

Through the mist of her tears, she had to smile, picturing the impossible erotic fantasies he had created for her. Who would have imagined Nick going to the trouble of making an Arabian Nights oasis on a New Jersey beach? Or the Senior Prom dream—come-true? Or the Highway Sex Scene?

Hmmm. A pattern began to emerge in Paula's mind. What was the big lug up to here? Was it merely seduction, trying to get her back? Or something more?

Well, she had more important things to discuss with him now. How dare he call a prospective employer and try to undermine her job efforts? The interference reeked of his obsessive protectiveness. And she planned to put a stop to it *now.* Obviously, their divorce was the only way to convince him of her seriousness.

"Well, well, well. If it isn't Mrs. Dickhead—I mean, Mrs. DiCello. I saw that asshole cop driving this bug . . . uh, car off the lot last week."

Paula was jarred from her deep thoughts by the drawling remark of a youth with a red bandanna tied around his head, gang style. He couldn't have been more than fourteen years old, but the deadness of his dark eyes bespoke no youthful innocence.

"Kindly step away from my car," Paula demanded, refusing

to show her fear. He half sat on the hood, his long, jeans-clad legs crossed at the ankles, his arms folded over his chest.

Paula wanted to scoot inside the protection of her car's interior—not that the tiny VW, with its soft top, would give her much protection. Oh, Lord, she wished she'd driven that damned, practically bulletproof Volvo. Pretending a nonchalance she didn't feel, she sidled around to the driver's side, but the boy straightened ominously and stepped in front of her.

"Where you goin', pretty lady?" he crooned, reaching out an arm and pulling the rubber band from her pony tail. Her hair spilled out around her shoulders. She tried to knock his hand aside, and his fingers locked on her wrist. "What's that mark on your neck, baby? Your hubby been givin' you hickeys, huh? I didn't think the old man had it in 'im. Maybe the dick has some lead in his pipe, after all."

His two friends, whom Paula just noticed leaning against a concrete wall, laughed at the crude joke.

He jerked on her wrist and pulled her closer. Paula could smell the musk of body odor and danger on his sweat-coated skin. "I think I got me a fine piece of tail here."

She struggled, in vain, and he laughed, enjoying her fear. Raising her other hand, she tried to swing her heavy purse at him, but one of his friends came up from behind and grabbed it, handing it to a third boy, who began to rummage through its contents.

"We gonna do a train on her, Lewis?" the boy behind her asked, rubbing his hips against her bottom, pressing her closer to Lewis, who was now propped against the driver's door, holding the soft flesh of her upper arms in an iron grip against her rib cage. She was now sandwiched between the two hoodlums.

Lewis leered at her and thrust his crotch toward her. "Yeah, I think this slut would enjoy a gang bang."

She gasped.

He grinned evilly. "Then we're gonna mark her up a bit. I warned DiCello. Maybe this time he'll lis—"

"Maybe this time *you'll* listen, Lewis. Man, we don't need this kinda shit. Let the lady go," a harsh, unfamiliar voice shouted behind her. Paula looked over her shoulder to see a gangly, black-haired boy approaching with two friends. They all wore the same red bandannas. And they were wielding ominous-looking knives.

"Stay out of this, Casale. This ain't your problem." Lewis stepped away from the car, still holding on to Paula's upper arm. The other hand pulled a knife from the waistband of his jeans.

Paula's heart thudded madly. With a spurt of adrenalin, she pulled out of his grasp. But immediately he backhanded her across the face, and she landed against the hood of her car, jarring her hip painfully. She tasted blood on her cut lip.

"Don't move," he warned, "or you're dead."

Paula could see that he was serious. He would have no compunction at all about killing her. So she remained still and watched in horror as the six boys, three against three, circled each other.

They struggled, slicing at each other with wary attacks and withdrawals. Harsh, vicious curses and ethnic slurs were thrown into the otherwise silent street. Threats of dire consequences if one or the other didn't back down.

In the end, they seemed to realize they were evenly matched, and there were going to be no easy winners. The fight was over in seconds. Both sides backed away, not surrendering, just putting off the outcome for another day. It appeared there would be no mortal wounds struck today.

Paula exhaled on a deep sigh.

Lewis bolted with his two friends, calling over his shoulder, "I'm gonna get you for this, Casale. And you, too, Mrs. DiCello. I'm coming after you both."

Casale's two friends chased after Lewis, but Paula's rescuer stayed behind. Not out of any concern for her, she realized immediately. He was bent over at the waist in pain, bleeding from a thigh wound, and his bare arms and neck bore minor slice marks from the deadly knives.

"Get in the car," she ordered. "I'm taking you to a hospital."

"It ain't nothin'. And I'm not goin' to no friggin' hospital. Just go."

Paula clucked at his false bravado and looked about for her purse. It was gone, of course. Well, at least, she still had her car keys in her skirt pocket. She unlocked the passenger door and pushed the youth inside. He was too weak to protest.

Quickly, she scanned the now empty street and walked around the front of the car. Soon she had the car in gear and was driving out of the city toward the hospital.

"I told you, I ain't goin' to no hospital. Besides, I just need to stop the bleeding. I've had worse than this lots of times." The boy had torn open the rip in his jeans, exposing a six-inch cut that was already coagulating. The cut couldn't be very deep. Pulling the dirty bandanna off his head, he wrapped it around the wound and winced.

"Well, it will have to be cleaned, and you need an antiseptic. Where's your house? I'll drive you there. Then we'll go to the police to report this crime."

The boy shot her a look of disbelief. "Are you nuts? I'm not goin' anywhere near my . . . place. Lewis will be on the lookout for me. And the police . . . hell, I ain't gonna squeal to no pigs."

Paula started to protest, then decided that taking care of his wound was the most important thing. Looking down at the key ring in the ignition, she realized that she still had the keys to Nick's apartment—the ones he'd given her a year ago in hopes they could reconcile. Making a quick decision, she said, "We'll go to Nick's place. It's nearby. Then *we* can decide what to do. What's your name, by the way?"

"Casale."

"No, I mean your first name."

The boy jerked his head toward her in surprise. At first, he balked, then he admitted in a soft voice, "Richie."

"Well, Richie," she said, turning to him as she pulled to a stop at a red light, "I want you to know that you are my hero. And I'm going to make damn sure no one hurts you again."

He glanced at her as if she'd really flipped her lid. "Me, a hero? No way! And there ain't nothin' you can do to protect me."

"Wanna bet?" She flashed him a secretive smile. Then she

ruffled his hair and leaned over to brush a kiss on his adolescent-fuzzy cheek.

He blushed and turned toward his side window, but Paula could have sworn she saw tears in his eyes.

She noticed the oddest thing then. On his left shoulder, just under the strap of his tank top, a blue-and-yellow tattoo peeked out, and it looked an awful lot like that sunflower tattoo she'd seen on Nick last night.

"Where did you get that tattoo?" she asked hesitantly.

He made a low growl of disgust. "Some broad out on Highway 10 talked me into it. I thought she was givin' me a skull, but instead, I got a damn flower. Geez! Can you believe it?"

Right now, Paula was beginning to believe anything was possible.

Chapter Nine

The puzzle pieces were finally coming together . . .

"TAKE OFF YOUR jeans, Richie."

"No way! I don't take off my pants for no chick unless I'm gonna boff her." The embarrassed boy raised his chin stubbornly and plopped back down on the closed lid of the toilet in Nick's pathetically tiny bathroom.

Paula thought about telling Richie that, at his age, the only "boffing" he did was in his dreams, but then she bit her tongue. These days, the sad fact was that even outside the ghetto kids engaged in sex at fourteen.

"Listen, sweetie, I've got to clean and disinfect your cut. I can't do it through that little rip in your jeans. I promise I won't look anywhere else. You can cover yourself."

He agreed finally, but he did put a towel over himself, just in case his "assets" were too much of a temptation for her. Luckily, his wounds proved only superficial, although painful, as evidenced by the boy's tight fists and tear-filled eyes.

"Now take a shower," she said gruffly, touched by his bravery. "And put these clean clothes on," she added, shoving a bundle into his hands. "You'll feel better."

A half hour later, Paula sat out on Nick's minuscule, third-floor balcony with Richie. He wore an old Adidas T-shirt of Nick's, along with a pair of his cutoffs, which were way too big, hanging down below his skinny knees.

Her heart went out to the barefooted youth, who continued to be awestruck at being in Detective DiCello's home, meager as it was. Shifting nervously in the porch chair, he could have been any other boy in the suburbs, not the dangerous gang member she'd witnessed earlier that day.

In fact, with his too-long black hair and blue eyes, he looked an awful lot like Nick might have at that age. *I wonder what Nick's son would look like . . . our son. Now that's a dangerous train of thought.*

She smiled then, watching Richie wolf down his second bowl of SpaghettiOs, washed down with a third glass of cherry Kool-Aid. *Blech!* How could Nick eat this swill? It was the only food she'd been able to find in his apartment, aside from a six-pack of beer and a carton of milk in the fridge, a box of Froot Loops in the cupboard, and four cans of unopened cat food in the trash can.

Speaking of cats . . . Paula looked down at the monster cat sitting imprisoned on her lap, hissing and glaring at Richie for daring to consume what she seemed to consider her personal supply of SpaghettiOs and Kool-Aid.

After all she'd learned that morning from Mrs. Chancellor, Paula now understood Nick's aversion to cats. They must remind him of his horrendous childhood in the projects and the tragic way in which his little sister had died.

Then why did Nick suddenly decide to get a cat?

The answer came to her instantly. *He wanted to please me. He wanted to show me that he's trying to change.* Paula's throat tightened with tenderness for her hard-boiled husband—a real pussycat at heart.

And she had a few other things to consider, as well. She'd almost been raped, and possibly killed, this morning. Those hoodlums had apparently threatened Nick that they would go after his wife. Perhaps other criminals he'd caught had done so, as well. In fact, he probably saw a whole lot of dangers out there every day in his police work, *real dangers,* and he had legitimate cause to take extraordinary precautions about her safety.

Could Nick's overprotectiveness these past few years have been warranted?

No!

Well, maybe.

Oh, she wasn't saying he hadn't gone too far, but maybe . . . hmmm . . . maybe she needed to rethink some things about Nick. And herself.

Just then, Richie laid the empty bowl on the patio table, and the cat made a quick, screeching leap for it.

Assuming the cat was about to attack him, Richie jerked back abruptly, causing his half-empty glass of Kool-Aid to fall from his hand to the concrete floor where it splintered apart.

"Oh, Mrs. DiCello, I'm sorry. Let me—" The horrified boy jumped from his chair and picked up a large sliver of glass.

"No, step back, Richie. You'll cut your bare feet," she warned. She went down on her haunches to pick up the remainder of the glass. Meanwhile, the stupid cat sat on the table, licking the SpaghettiOs bowl clean.

"Get up, Mrs. DiCello. Or you're gonna get cut, real bad."

His worst fear was realized . . .

NICK WAS IN A frenzy as he approached his apartment door. An anonymous caller had alerted police to an attack on his wife earlier that day, hanging up before the desk sergeant could ask for details on whether Paula was safe or injured. He, and practically every police officer and detective in his unit, had spent the past few hours trying to locate her, to no avail.

Finally, Captain O'Malley had sent him home to shower and calm down before returning to the station. "You're not doing anyone any good, going off half-cocked like this, least of all Paula," O'Malley had told him. "Don't come back till you can think rationally."

Hah! I'll never be able to think rationally while Paula is still out there. Maybe raped. Or wounded. Or dead. No! I won't believe the worst until I find her. I've got to think she's okay. I've got to. Otherwise—

Nick stopped dead in mid-thought. A sixth sense rang like a bell inside his head. Something didn't feel right. He turned the key in his lock, and the door pushed open. Too easily.

It wasn't locked. Unlike Paula, he never left a door unlocked. Never.

"Hell!" Reflexively, he reached under his jacket and unbuckled his shoulder holster. Pulling out his gun, he moved toward the balcony where he heard Paula's voice. *Thank God!*

Well, that explained the unlocked door. It appeared Paula's lack of concern over safety would never change.

He started to put his gun back in the holster, then hesitated when he heard a loud crash, like glass breaking. Then Paula's voice. Who was Paula talking to? And in such a frantic tone of voice?

"Get up, Mrs. DiCello. Or you're gonna get cut, real bad," he heard a male voice say.

Oh, God! As he approached the open balcony door, he saw Paula down on her knees and some punk leaning over her with a deadly shard of broken glass in his fingers. His heart stopped, with a lurch, and a loud roaring exploded in his ears. The weapon dripped a red substance onto the back of her white blouse.

Blood! Oh, no! Paula's blood!

Then he noticed her face. Fingermarks formed welts on her one cheek, and her upper lip appeared to be cut and slightly swollen.

A boiling haze of fury threatened to blind Nick for that brief second before he assumed a firing position. Drawing his weapon, he spread his legs, dropped into a slight crouch, and took aim, wrapping all ten fingers around the handle. With one finger over the trigger, he pointed at the perp's back, dead center.

"*Freeze!*" he yelled in warning. "Police!"

The guy turned with surprise, then stared at him wide-eyed with fear, his eyes riveted on the gun in Nick's hands.

Casale? What the hell is Casale doing attacking my wife?

Nick lowered his gun momentarily in surprise, then raised it again. "Drop your weapon, boy. Slowly. Or . . . you . . . are . . . dead. And, believe me, you slime-ball, it will give me great pleasure to be the one to off you."

"Nick, are you crazy? Put that gun away. *Now!*" Paula stood and glared at him.

"Move over here, Paula. It's okay now. He can't hurt you anymore."

Instead of obeying his orders, his contrary wife stepped in

front of Casale, protecting him with outspread arms.

"Move, Paula. This isn't a game. It's—"

"I'll tell you what it is, you jerk," she snapped angrily. "It's a big misunderstanding. This boy saved my life today, and you almost killed him. Are you nuts?"

"Saved your life?" he repeated numbly.

"Yes, he chased away some gang members who tried to attack me, and he got hurt in the process. He didn't want to go to the hospital, and your apartment was closer than mine. So I brought him here." She took in a big swallow of air after her long-winded explanation.

"But the blood . . .?" He glanced down at the puddle on the balcony floor.

"Blood?" She tilted her head with confusion, then made a clucking sound of disgust. "Cherry Kool-Aid, you fool."

"Kool . . . Kool-Aid! But . . . how about those bruises on your face?"

"Lewis backhanded her," Casale interjected.

"Lewis?" Nick blinked as understanding seeped into his thick head, and his heart slowed down to about a hundred and fifty beats per second. He lowered the gun and sank into a nearby chair, his hands shaking visibly. He laid his gun on the table. "Holy hell! You scared the hell out of me today, Paula," he said on a loud exhale.

"I scared *you*? Why, you big doofus! Look what you've done to this boy."

Reluctantly, he raised his eyes to Casale, who looked as if he might have wet his shorts with fright. Then Nick's eyes widened in surprise as he noticed something else. The kid was wearing *his* cut-off shorts. And his T-shirt, too.

Oh, Lord.

"I better go," Casale said, inching his way toward the apartment door.

"No!" Nick shouted.

Both Casale and Paula jumped.

"I mean, I want you to stay. I'm sorry if I overreacted—"

"Overreacted?" Paula snorted. "You almost killed an innocent boy. I'd say that's a hell of a lot worse than overreaction."

Nick winced at her harsh appraisal.

"Sit down, Richie," he said, more softly, deliberately using his given name. "Please. We need to talk."

After a half hour in which Paula and Richie explained what had happened that morning, and Nick told them of his frantic search for her after the anonymous tip, they all relaxed a bit.

While Nick reported in to the police station, Richie ate what Paula told Nick, with a raised eyebrow, was a third can of his SpaghettiOs and the last of his cherry Kool-Aid. He sensed one of her nutrition lectures coming later.

Finally, he told Richie, "C'mon, kid."

"Nick, you can't take him home. Those other gang members will look for him there."

"Paula, this kid doesn't have a home."

"What . . . what do you mean?"

"He lives in a shelter, or the street."

"How'd you know that, man?"

"I know *everything* about you, my friend." Nick turned back to Paula, continuing, "His dad took off a long time ago, and his mother's in prison for theft and possession and sale of a controlled substance."

"And prostitution," Richie added in a flat voice.

Paula gasped, raising tear-filled eyes helplessly to Nick. "On the streets? Homeless?"

"Don't worry," he assured his wife. "I'm gonna take him someplace where he'll be safe."

"Where?" Richie demanded. "I ain't goin' to no juvie hall."

"No, I'm not taking you to a reformatory," he said, ruffling Richie's hair with sudden affection. His throat choked up as he realized the punk had saved his wife's life. He owed him big time. "Richie, I'm going to find a better place for you. Just like someone did for me a long time ago. Like I should have done for you before . . ." He felt a huge lump of emotion grow in his throat, and he couldn't continue.

But Paula and Richie stood with arms folded over their chests stubbornly, refusing to budge.

"Okay, I made a few calls after I booked you the last time," he explained to the boy. "There's this program called The Last Chance that places inner city kids in foster care programs. In fact, I already talked to some people about a vacancy in their residence in Spruce Valley, Vermont. They have a home with resident house parents for boys from inner cities. It's run by that former Olympic runner Jerry Vandermeer."

Both Paula and Richie listened with furrowed brows to his long explanation.

"So?" Richie asked finally, trying to sound coolly indifferent, but clearly interested.

"So, it would give you a chance to live in a normal home atmosphere, out of the ghetto. Maybe even go to college someday. Hell, this could be your ticket to a better life, boy. Are you interested?"

Richie shuffled his feet. "I ain't never been outside Newark. Are there cows and stuff there? I ain't never even seen a real cow."

Nick pressed his lips together to stifle a smile. "Spruce Valley is a fairly big town, but there might be a cow or two on the outskirts."

"And you say you lived in one of these places once?"

Nick nodded, ignoring Paula's surprised expression.

Fear and hope fought a battle on Richie's open face. Hope won out. "Maybe."

"All right. I'm going to take you over to the home of a friend of mine, George Madison. He acts as a liaison with The Last Chance. You can stay there tonight, and tomorrow someone will drive you to Spruce Valley to visit." Nick turned to Paula then. "Does that meet with your approval?"

She didn't have to answer. The tears in her eyes spoke volumes.

"I'll be back in an hour. And you"—he pointed a finger at his stubborn wife—"stay right here. Don't move from this apartment till I get back. We have some major talking to do, babe."

"Babe? You call your wife 'babe'?" Richie snickered. "Cool!

I didn't think old people did that." Then his eyes almost bugged out as he looked at something behind Nick. "Wow!"

Nick turned, and his eyes did bug out. His damn cat was sprawled, big as you please, on his favorite easy chair in the living room. Popping out baby cats.

Paula helped him make the cat more comfortable and had to tell him at least ten times to stop swearing in front of the boy. *Hah!* As if Richie couldn't teach him a few blue words!

"Hell, what am I going to do with five cats? Oh, no! There comes another one. Geez! I won't be able to breathe. There'll be cat hair everywhere. I'll go broke buying SpaghettiOs. Bet there's lice on—"

"Shut up, Nick," she said softly. "I'll help you find a home for them. Relax."

"Easy for you to say," he muttered.

The last straw came when he was walking out of the apartment with his arm looped over the kid's shoulder, and Paula called out, "Nick, did you know that Richie has a tattoo just like yours?"

"Huh?" He glanced down to where Richie's stretched neckband had slipped over to one side. He burst out laughing. It was probably delayed hysteria.

A sunflower stood out like a beacon on Richie's shoulder. Just like Nick's.

The kid looked at him in question. "Whoa! You have a sunflower tattoo, too?"

Nick nodded, with a sick feeling in the pit of his stomach. "Madame Nadine, right?"

"Yep," Richie said and grinned. "She said it would bring me good luck. She said there was going to be a dark stranger coming to save me, like one of those old knights, and—" He gaped at Nick suddenly, as if he'd sprouted a suit of shining armor.

"Hell!" Nick exclaimed.

"That's what I said to Madame Nadine." Then Richie seemed to think of something else. "I don't s'pose you got a horse?"

"No, just a cat that looks like a horse."

Before he closed the door, making sure to secure the locks, he heard Paula laugh and add, "Don't forget the camel."

Chapter Ten

Being a hero sucks . . .

AFTER TAKING Richie to George Madison's house, Nick spent some time reassuring the boy that everything would be okay. Actually, Richie and George, a young guidance counselor at a nearby private school, hit it off great. Nick had a good feeling about Richie and his future.

His own future was a lot more shaky.

Nick decided to take the long way home. Thinking. Making decisions.

He'd almost killed an innocent boy today. And that had taught him a screeching big lesson.

He felt like a monster, a cripple, handicapped by his overwhelming need to screen his wife from the dark side of life.

Paula was right. He was obsessed with her safety.

Hell, life was dangerous everywhere today. Even in the suburbs. Even in rural America. He'd been looking for guarantees where none existed. People couldn't live behind barred windows to avoid danger, the way he'd been trying to do with Paula. That was no way to survive. No way to live.

How could I have been so blind? Over and over he berated himself with that question as he drove aimlessly.

The big question was, could he change?

Unfortunately, the answer was no. At least, not in the big ways that would matter most to Paula.

I'm going to have to let Paula go, he decided finally.

His heart ached at the thought, and tears welled in his eyes, but Paula had been right about another thing, too. Sometimes, real love meant letting go. As much as it hurt, that was just what Nick resolved to do. For Paula.

I'm going to have to be a hero. Nick laughed cynically at the prospect.

It won't be so bad, he tried to tell himself. *I could always quit my job, give up my dismal excuse for an apartment, and move to the Bahamas. Become a beach bum. Drink beer all the time. Learn to surf.*

He tried to smile, but all he could manage was a grimace.

Hey, I know, I could become a private detective and ask Madame Nadine to go into business with me. We could call ourselves The Psycho Detective Agency.

No, no, no! I've got it. I'll locate that codger from the bookstore, and we'll write a sex advice book together. Sex For the Brain-Challenged, *or, better yet,* Screwing for Screw-ups.

A lump of despair the size of a cantaloupe lodged in his throat. Probably a hair ball.

Speaking of cats. I could always become a cat breeder. He shuddered with distaste. Now, that wasn't even funny.

Finally, two hours later, Nick let himself into his apartment. He didn't even curse when the door opened too easily. Apparently, Paula had disobeyed his orders to stay put. As usual.

The smells of good home cooking permeated the air. Paula must have gone to the grocery store.

He sniffed appreciatively, leaning back against the door with closed eyes. Marinara sauce. That probably meant angel hair pasta. He sniffed again. Bacon. Aaah! Spinach salad with hot bacon dressing. Two of his favorites.

This is going to be a lot harder than I thought.

"Nick, is that you?"

"No, it's Jack the Ripper. And you left the door unlocked for him."

"Oh." There was a long pause, then she said weakly, "I guess I forgot . . . again."

She stepped out of the kitchen.

And his knees buckled.

He braced one hand on the wall for support. His shattered nerves had sustained a number of shocks today. Apparently, the bumpy road was far from over.

Paula was wearing scanty, cream-colored silk tap pants and

a matching camisole edged in lace. And that was all.

He gulped. *Yep, this is going to be a whole lot harder than I thought.*

The racy undergarments were intended to be the ingredients for Fantasy Number Four. Well, that was out of the question now.

She smiled shyly at him and laid some napkins on the table, which she'd placed invitingly before the balcony door. Even a tablecloth had appeared from somewhere. Son of a gun! His tiny apartment looked almost presentable. *Maybe I won't move to the Bahamas and drink beer, after all. I can wallow right here in comfort.*

Then he noticed her toenails. *Pink! She painted her toenails pink. Oh, that's a low blow. She knows how I love her toes, especially in pink polish. I am in bi-i-g trouble!*

Get a grip, DiCello, he told himself. *Your brain is splintering apart.*

"I found these clothes in some Victoria's Secret boxes in your bedroom. I couldn't resist trying them on. I assumed . . . I mean, I probably shouldn't have . . . but I assumed they were for me." Her face flamed with embarrassment.

He should tell her they belonged to someone else. He should say he'd bought them for another woman. "They're for you," he said gruffly, moving closer. "Along with all the sexy things in those other boxes."

She raised an eyebrow at him. "More of your middle-aged sexual fantasy stuff?"

"Yep." He furrowed his brow suspiciously. What was Paula up to here?

Well, whatever it was, he would have to resist. He would have to push her away. Be a hero.

But the unheroic side of his brain disagreed. It forced him to grin, loop a forefinger under one of the tiny straps at her shoulder, and tug, closing the gap between them.

The lemony fragrance of her perfume wafted around him, enticing his senses. *Okay, I know I've got to be a hero, but there's nothing in the hero code that says I can't enjoy the smells before taking off into the sunset.*

His gaze shifted back to her scandalous attire. "A perfect fit, I see." *Or the view. There's nothing wrong with a hero looking . . . one last time.*

"Uh-huh." Her lips parted, and she stared up at him through sultry, half-lidded eyes.

His noble decision to let Paula go weighed heavily on him. Being a hero was proving to be real tough. He backed up a step, his eyes narrowing suspiciously. "What are you up to, Paula?"

"Up to? Me?" She batted her lashes at him with mock innocence, then added, "Who did you send into the store to buy this stuff? One of the female detectives?" She began to stalk him. Closer and closer.

He took another step backward, around the table. "I picked them all out myself, babe," he said in a wounded voice. "And I didn't need to ask anyone about sizes, either." He looked her over meaningfully. "I have a perfect memory."

She laughed, a delightful, joyous sound that rippled over his parched soul like rain in the desert.

"You? A macho guy like you traipsing around in a lingerie store? I find that hard to believe," she scoffed, but Nick could see that she was pleased.

He felt confused and disoriented, barely able to follow their conversation.

Yep, this is going to be a whole helluva lot harder than I expected.

He steeled himself to be strong and deliberately put the table between them. "One of the clerks asked me if I'd like her to model that outfit," he said, his eyes feasting on her skimpy, delicious attire. It was best if he went for a light mood. It was best if he didn't even look at his wife. It was best if he got the hell out of there.

"I'll bet she did," Paula snapped. Jealousy turned her cheeks pink with chagrin.

He liked that. "But I told her I'd rather see my *wife* do the modeling."

Paula blinked rapidly at him.

"Don't you dare cry."

"I'm not crying." She wiped her eyes, nonetheless, and asked, "Is Richie okay?"

Now, this was safe territory. "Yeah. I'll stop by to see him again tomorrow before he leaves. In fact . . . well, I was thinking . . . maybe I'll drive up to see him in a couple of days."

She nodded. "Maybe I'll go with you."

"How about the damn cat?" he asked, floundering for neutral subjects. *Yep, it is definitely best to change the subject. And what better way to cool my ardor than talk about cats.* "How many kittens do I have to blackmail my friends into taking?" he asked, concerned about Gargoyle and her progeny, despite himself.

"Seven. And the mother is just fine." She pointed to a corner of the living room where a large wicker cat bed was situated with the happy family firmly ensconced. Nearby, a litter box stood ready. He raised an eyebrow. Apparently, Paula had done more than a little shopping in his absence.

Then her words sank in. "Seven! I don't know enough people I hate enough to foist seven cats on."

"Now, Nick, I know you don't really mean that."

"Don't bet the farm on it, babe. How soon can I take Gargoyle back to Madame Nadine?"

"You're still going to take her back?" she asked in surprise. "I thought maybe you two had bonded by now."

"Bonded? Are you nuts? I'd rather bond with a barrel of Krazy Glue."

Paula smiled and sashayed around the table. That was the only way to describe the swish and sway of her hips in the revealing tap pants.

He forgot to move. When he did, belatedly, the back of his knees hit the seat of a straight-backed chair. He plopped down.

"Paula, we have to talk about . . ." he started to say.

At the same time, she said, "Nick, honey, I want to thank you . . ."

Honey? Uh-oh! "Listen, Paula, I've finally realized . . . huh? What do you have to thank me for?"

"For taking care of Richie. He's a good kid. He reminds me of you."

"Hah! No way!" But secretly, now that he thought about it, he agreed. "Besides, it's my job. Actually, it's kind of nice to be able to help a kid once in a while. Mostly, I just lock them up."

"Oh, Nick."

"Don't start feeling sorry for me, Paula. And stop changing the subject. About the divorce. I've decided . . ." He gulped, having trouble spitting out the words.

"Later, sweetheart. Right now . . . are you hungry?"

"What?"

She didn't give him a chance to answer. Instead, she moved in for the kill. With the ease of a siren, she slipped onto his lap, straddling his legs. Looping her arms around his neck, she asked huskily, "Well?"

"Huh?"

"Are you hungry?"

"Oh, yeah."

She squirmed her silk-clad bottom up higher on his lap, and he felt fireworks ignite all over his body. In fact, his rocket practically left the launch pad.

He tried to remember his earlier resolve. Their marriage was over. He was going to let her go. He was going to be a hero.

"Take off your jacket and shirt, Nick," she coaxed as she nibbled his cheek and neck. "Your gun is poking me."

"Which gun?" he choked out, feeling like he was about to explode.

One side of his brain said he should fight his baser urges as Paula laughed seductively and helped him slip out of his coat. His conscience screamed, *Get up and walk out the door. It's over between me and Paula. It has to be.*

But the other, stronger side of his brain argued, *Well, maybe there could be one last time.*

Sighing in surrender, he unbuckled his holster and let it slide to the floor, then watched with fascination as Paula unbuttoned his shirt, pressing gentle kisses along the path of his exposed chest.

He groaned. "I'm trying to be a hero here, Paula," he protested half-heartedly.

"You *are* my hero, Nick."

"Oh, great! Make me feel guilty. Paula . . . could you stop touching me *there,* babe . . . listen . . . I don't believe you just did *that* . . . oh, Lord . . . oh, Lord, this is not a good idea."

"Honey, this is the best idea I've had all day. In fact, all week. Maybe even all year." She moved her hips against him, and he almost shot out of the chair. "Don't move," she ordered. "Just let me . . ."

She looked at him through dreamy green eyes, and he knew he was lost.

With a knowing smile, she placed a fingertip on the pulse point in his neck, and his heartbeat accelerated.

She fingered the edges of his hair, brushed his collarbone, stroked his bare arms. And he made a hissing sound of surrender.

Gently, he rocked his hips forward, and a mewling cry of sweet surprise escaped her parted lips. To his satisfaction, her long lashes fluttered uncontrollably.

Pleasure flooded through him in a violent shiver. He felt like he was catapulting through space. His body ached from scalp to toe.

She put her hands on either side of his face, gently, and pressed her lips to his, whispering throatily, "Nick."

Just "Nick."

But that one word shattered any resistance he had left. His mouth opened under hers, taking her tempting tongue. He grew against her.

She drew back slightly. For a brief second, the intense physical awareness resonated between them as their eyes held.

Okay, so I'll be a hero a half hour from now. Hah! Who am I kidding? Ten minutes from now. Then he placed her hand over his sex. He almost passed out from the bone-melting waves of sweet heat that licked over him. He was barely aware that Paula was undoing his belt buckle and unzipping his fly. He watched helplessly as she took him in one hand and used the other to push aside the wide leg of her panties. With a long, drawn-out sigh, she raised herself slightly, then eased down, inch by excruciating inch, onto his erection until he was buried in her hot center.

"Pau-la," he ground out, putting his wide palms on her buttocks to hold her in place. When the first turbulent wave of his arousal had passed, he leaned down and kissed her taut nipples through the silk camisole. Her head reared back, and she began to whimper.

"Now," he said, still embedded in her.

She nodded and slowly undulated her hips. Expertly, her slick sheath stroked him, building the fires of his molten desire.

He wanted to make it last forever.

It was over in minutes.

But they were the best damn minutes of his life.

Breathing raggedly, he wrapped his arms around her waist and feathered kisses over her lips and neck and shoulders, whispering soft endearments between each kiss. His love flowed over them both, and her eyes grew large and liquid with emotion.

When he felt himself begin to thicken again, he stood abruptly, with Paula still riding his sex, and laid her on the table, sweeping aside the placemats and napkins. He climbed up with her and reached down and behind to grip her ankles and pull them up and out. This time, his body hammered its need into her welcoming folds. Penetrating deep, he used his body to show her how very much he loved her.

When the first tingles of his impending climax flash-flooded through his body, he laced his fingers with hers, holding her to the table, and pummeled her with rapid-fire, mind-blowing strokes. Her eyes gazed up at him, unfocused and misty with passion. She made soft, mewling sounds of entreaty, "Please, Nick . . . oh, no . . . oh, yes . . . now . . . *now!*"

He slammed into her one last time, crying out his triumphant release.

And she wrapped her legs around his waist, yielding to the uncontrollable convulsions of her own climax which alternately clasped and unclasped his sex.

When he was finally able to breathe, he rolled off Paula and tucked her under his arm. He kissed her softly, smiling against her lips. "That was some appetizer, babe."

She slanted him a look of disbelief, then answered saucily, "Wait till you see what I have for the main course."

That was when he remembered his good intentions. There

was going to be no main course for them.

But Paula had other intentions.

And Nick's willpower seemed to have taken a leave of absence, he learned, as Paula served him one delicious "main course" after another, each wrapped in a different Victoria's Secret outfit. Nick swore he was going to buy stock in the company first thing Monday morning.

About 2:00 A.M., they finally decided to eat dinner.

"Nick, why is that sock sitting on the kitchen counter?" Paula said as she prepared to put the food on the table.

"It's my potholder," he said distractedly as he soaked in the remarkable view of Paula in a red-and-black bustier and garter belt, bent over the oven where a loaf of garlic bread was warming.

"A potholder!" she exclaimed, peering up at him over her shoulder. She tsked her disapproval when she noticed the target of his perusal—her nicely curved derriere.

"I haven't had a chance to shop lately," he said sheepishly.

She made another tsking sound and placed the bread on the table alongside the pasta and salad. She motioned him to sit down and commented idly, "And how come your Jockey shorts look so gray? Not to mention the sheets and dish towels."

"Shampoo." He was already helping himself to a generous serving of the food, realizing belatedly that he hadn't eaten all day.

"Shampoo?" Paula blinked at him with confusion.

"Yeah. I ran out of soap powder, so I've been using shampoo in the washing machine. Lord, you should have seen all the bubbles. The building manager told me he's gonna sue me if I ever do it again." He was eating ravenously the whole time he talked. Finally, he glanced up when he noticed the silence. "What? Why are you looking at me like that?"

"Oh, Nick."

"Now what? You look like you're gonna cry. Just because I ran out of soap powder?"

"Because I lo—"

"Hey, it's no big deal," he interrupted in a panic. He

couldn't let her finish. He just couldn't. He wanted to believe there was still a chance for them, but he was afraid to hope. And he didn't want to break this precious bond that connected them tonight.

He searched his brain for a way to change the subject. "Geez, if that's what turns you on, maybe I should tell you what I've been using for a toilet brush."

She stared at him incredulously, then laughed. "I don't think I want to know."

"You know, Skip passes on the best tips to me."

"I can imagine."

"Betcha didn't know what you can do with the crumbs at the bottom of a toaster."

"Throw them away?" she suggested.

"Nah, they make great croutons."

They exchanged a smile. Nick wished he could freeze the moment and make time stand still. "God help me," he murmured under his breath.

When they returned to the bedroom, Nick undressed her slowly, worshipfully. With each garment that slid off her body to the carpet, his lips followed the silken path, whispering soft words of appreciation at the beauty of her smooth skin, the sensitivity of her breasts, the flatness of her stomach, the length of her legs.

Dropping his shorts, he stood before her, inhaling her lemony cologne. "Do you know that I bought a sack of lemons one day and squeezed them in bowls all over the apartment just to remind me of you?" he disclosed as he ran the pad of his thumb over her parted lips.

She leaned closer. "Oh, honey, I—"

"And once I went into Saks and had the clerk take out one perfume sample after another, trying to find yours."

A sad smile curved her mouth. "It's Jean Naté cologne. They sell it in the drugstore, silly. Not Saks." She reached up a hand to cup the side of his face.

He took her hand in his and kissed the palm, then the wrist. He felt her pulse jump against his lips.

Feeling dizzy and intoxicated, Nick led his wife to the bed. Frozen in a limbo of love and pure physical sensation, he pushed all logic aside and wanted to believe that anything was possible.

He would never forget a single detail of this night. *Never!*

Forcing her to remain immobile on her back, he paid homage to her body, from scalp to toe.

"Lie still, hon. Let me do the work," he implored huskily against the soft curve of her throat.

"But Nick—"

"Shhh." His lips moved lower and covered one breast.

"Oooooh, my God!" she keened and arched her chest up off the bed.

He suckled rhythmically.

And she began to make low, whimpering gasps of need.

He smiled and drew back, examining the wet nipple appreciatively.

"Don't stop," she cried out.

He moved to the other breast obediently. "As if I ever could!" he said against the hot, turgid flesh.

By the time he had traveled the slow, slow journey over her responsive body, giving particular attention to the shadowy curve under her arms, the dip of her navel, the backs of her knees, even her delicious toes, Paula was writhing from side to side, begging him to end her torment. "Now, Nick. I want you *now.*"

She tried to reach up for him, but he pushed her back gently and knelt between her outspread thighs. "Uh-uh, babe," he asserted with a low growl. Placing his palms under her buttocks, he lifted her up off the mattress and nuzzled her hair. "You've been providing me with one main course after another, sweetheart. It's time for a feast of another kind."

By the time they were both satisfied, Nick lay depleted on his back, his arms thrown over his head, his legs spread with satiety. Sweat coated both their slick bodies, and the only sounds in the deep night were those of their syncopated, ragged breaths.

He pulled Paula into the crook of his arm and kissed the top of her head. "That was sensational, honey."

"Yeah, it was, wasn't it?"

Paula raised herself slightly and brushed the hair off his forehead. "I know about your childhood, Nick."

An icy foreboding rippled over him. "What do you mean?"

"Mrs. Chancellor told me about your sister Lita . . . how she died. And about your brother in prison. Nick, why didn't you tell me? Maybe I would have understood you better. Maybe—"

All of Nick's newfound hopes for their future came crashing down. "Damn her! She had no right," Nick exclaimed, trying to push Paula to the side so he could get up.

She wouldn't let him. "I'm glad she did. At least now we have some logical point where we can start to communicate."

Pity . . . Paula had made love with him out of pity. And, oh, God, now she knew how he'd let his family down. How he'd fail her, too. Pain roiled in his head in angry waves. He couldn't think. "I don't want to talk about my past, or Lita, or the projects, or—"

"I know, I know, but we will. Tomorrow." She burrowed closer and chuckled softly.

"What's so funny? You think the things Mrs. Chancellor blabbed to you are humorous?"

"Of course not. I was just thinking that you must have learned a lot from all those books."

"What books?" Her change of subject puzzled him.

"When I was looking through those Victoria's Secret boxes, I saw that pile of books in the back of the closet. Since when are you into how-to sex books?"

Then he remembered. *Oops!* "Since I lost you."

She propped herself on one elbow and stared down at him. "You'd better explain that."

He told her all about Madame Nadine, and Paula's mouth dropped open. "You went to a fortune-teller to get advice on how to win me back? *You?*"

"Yeah. Dumb, wasn't I?" He felt his face turn hot. "But she's not just a fortune-teller. She also does tattoos. And other stuff." He rolled his eyes meaningfully, then told her about the character at the bookstore. She laughed till tears ran down her face.

He kissed them away.

Nestling at his side once again, she yawned and said, "So all these sexual fantasy events were at Madame Nadine's suggestion?"

"Well, not exactly. She told me I had to find your 'heart craving', and I punched in cravings at the bookstore computer, and it came back with all these sexual fantasy titles, and I thought . . ." His words trailed off as he realized how ridiculous they sounded. "Hey, it made sense at the time."

Paula shook her head hopelessly. "You jerk. The only craving I've ever had that you didn't meet was the need to be free of your obsessiveness."

"Free?" Nick felt like he'd been blindsided. "I thought you loved me."

"What does love have to do with it? You're my husband, not my jailer. A wife shouldn't feel like a prisoner."

"I didn't realize . . . you've been miserable, haven't you, Paula?"

"Very," she agreed with a yawn. "Freedom, that's all I ever wanted, but you wouldn't listen. I've been so unhappy for so long. I can't remember what it's like to feel happy—and free—anymore."

Paula didn't know how her words shattered him. She just burrowed closer and yawned again. "We must have a *long* talk in the morning, Nick. I see so many things differently now. You do, too. I know you do." And she fell instantly asleep.

But Nick didn't sleep at all that night. He kept thinking about her words, *I've been so unhappy for so long.*

Paula loved him. Nick knew that. And he loved her. Too damn much.

Well, it was time to prove that love.

Toward morning, with tears welling in his eyes, Nick kissed his sleeping wife one last time and rose from the bed. Minutes later, he signed a note, which he left for her on the table. Then he slipped out the door, unable to stop himself from double-checking the lock.

"Be happy, Paula," he whispered in a broken voice.

Chapter Eleven

Women can play fantasy games, too . . .

PAULA OVERSLEPT.

When she awakened, the warm sun already streamed through the open balcony door, portending another hot summer day. Maybe she could talk Nick into going to the beach house with her later. In fact, if he had any vacation time coming, they could spend the week there, sort of a second honeymoon.

She smiled and rolled over to the side, opening her eyes.

Nick was gone.

That wasn't really surprising, she decided, despite her disappointment. It must be close to 10:00 A.M., and he usually started his shift at nine. She *was* surprised that he hadn't awakened her to say good-bye, though. Well, he was only being considerate, she concluded.

Stretching languidly, she relished the ache of muscles that hadn't been exercised in a long time—until the past few days. Looking down, she saw whisker burns on her breasts, a bruise on her thigh, even a faint bite mark on her flat belly.

She felt an odd thrill, seeing those marks of Nick's fierce lovemaking on her skin. He'd been so hungry. For her. And that was a powerful compliment, in her opinion.

A hazy memory nagged at her of their conversation before she fell asleep. Something about his past and her heart craving.

But it was the strange, forlorn look on his face she remembered now. Hmmm. Shrugging, she figured it would all be cleared up today.

She swung her legs over the side of the bed. Today was going to be the first day of the rest of their lives *together*. That meant lots of work. She began to make a mental list.

Number one, of course, she and Nick had to talk. Clearly, they loved each other as much as ever. That was the most important thing.

Number two, she had to phone her lawyer and call off the divorce proceedings.

Number three, she and Nick would need to make arrangements to sublet his apartment and sell her condo. She wanted their new beginning to start in a home of *both* their choosing, not just his. Although she would insist on no bars on the windows, she was ready to compromise on some of his safety measures.

Number four, she would call Mrs. Chancellor and withdraw her job application. After her near escape yesterday, she saw the logic in Nick's concern for her safety. They'd both been at fault over the danger issue, but she could make concessions, if he could.

Suddenly Paula realized how much she'd learned the last few days about Nick and herself. His obsessiveness over her safety had forced her into a corner, but now she saw the reasons for his over-protectiveness.

And he had been trying to change. He really had.

To think that he'd actually gone to a fortune-teller for help! She grinned and shook her head hopelessly. How endearing it was that Nick had staged all those sexual fantasy events just to satisfy her "heart."

The fool! Didn't he know that the only thing her heart had ever craved was his love—an unconditional love, free of obsessiveness? The love had never died, for either of them, and she vowed that in the future there would be open lines of communication between them—no more secrets.

She determined to meet this Madame Nadine, too. She had a lot to thank her for, and not just that adorable cat, Gargoyle.

Okay, first things first. Coffee. She needed coffee to jumpstart the day.

After checking to make sure Gargoyle and her kittens were all right and supplied with fresh food and water, Paula headed for the kitchen. Grimacing with distaste, she began to wash last night's dirty dishes while her instant coffee heated in the microwave.

That was when she noticed the note on the table.

A tingle of foreboding swept her body as she walked closer. With trepidation, she picked it up.

She gasped and pressed one hand over her heart as she began to read.

> *Paula: I love you. Because of that love, I'm giving you your heart craving—your freedom. It's the hardest, most heroic thing I've ever done in my life. I won't be at the hearing today, but I've signed the papers for you.*
>
> *Be happy, babe. Just be happy.*
>
> *Love,*
>
> *Nick*

Tears welled in Paula's eyes and spilled over. *A hero? The jerk! Now, after all this time, he decides to be noble.*

Paula sobbed softly, but more for Nick than for herself. She knew how much Nick must love her to have signed these papers. She knew he'd done it for her. Hot tears burned her eyes, streaming down her cheeks.

They should have talked their problems out last night before falling asleep. But she'd been so confident that their marriage was over the biggest hurdle. Why couldn't Nick have understood, without the words?

He couldn't read her mind any more than she'd been able to read his all these years, she immediately chastised herself.

God, I love the man. And, God, how I'd like to whack some sense into his thick skull. He should have talked to me first! How long is it going to take him to learn that communication is our problem, not any "heart craving"?

Wiping the tears from her eyes with a tissue, she stood and lifted her chin resolutely. Oh, she wasn't going to let the numbskull go, but she decided he needed to be taught a lesson. Tapping a forefinger thoughtfully against her chin, she pondered all her choices.

Finally, she smiled.

After canceling the hearing with her lawyer, who was not surprised at all, she called Skip. He listened as she outlined her plan.

"Stop laughing, Skip. I'm serious."

"That's why I'm laughing."

"Are you going to help me?"

"Yeah, I guess so. Can I follow and watch?"

"No."

"Dammit, Paula, you guys are no fun. Nick wouldn't let me stay and watch you ride a camel, and—"

"I did not ride a camel," she said indignantly.

"—or model Jezebel's harem outfit."

Jezebel? I'm going to kill Nick. "Are you going to help me or not?"

"Okay, but I expect a full report from both of you. I can't wait to see what you two come up with next."

Yeah, me, too.

"Are you sure you don't want to try my idea of being a stripper at the club, and Nick an unsuspecting member of the audience? The owner still hasn't found a replacement for Lee."

"Maybe some other time."

But, officer, I really wasn't speeding . . . much . . .

NICK HAD GONE into work that morning, but one look at his ashen face and Captain O'Malley had sent him home. Of course, he couldn't go home yet. Paula would still be there, and he couldn't face her. Not today when their marriage would be ending.

Instead, he'd gone to Madison's house and talked to Richie for a long time. Over breakfast at McDonald's, he'd reassured the kid that moving out of the city would be the best thing, that it had worked for him. And he'd promised Richie that he could call him anytime, that he could consider him a friend.

After that, he'd driven to the projects and stood, leaning against his car in the parking lot, watching the everyday activities.

Nothing changed here in the ghetto. Nothing. But he should have put all this behind him long ago. Instead, he'd carried his past around like an albatross.

In a way, he was saying good-bye to his sister Lita, as well as Paula, today. The guilt had somehow slipped off his shoulders.

He looked at his watch and sighed. 1:45 P.M. The hearing was scheduled for 2:00 P.M. Another half hour, and he could go home to drink himself into numbness. Then tomorrow, he was going to have to learn how to live without Paula, one day at a time.

But first, he wanted to stop by Madame Nadine's and give her a piece of his mind. Some psychic she turned out to be!

Fifteen minutes later, Nick sat in his car along the highway, stunned.

There was no rundown yellow house. No sign that proclaimed, MADAME NADINE: FORTUNE TELLING, LOVE POTIONS, MIRACLES. And in smaller letters, HAIR WAXING AND TATTOOS, BY APPOINTMENT. No giant sunflowers. No herd of cats.

He hit the side of his head with the heel of his palm and looked again. Nothing. Just an empty lot overgrown with knee-high weeds.

He saw a jogger approaching and rolled down the passenger window. "Hey, buddy, what happened to the house that was here yesterday?"

The middle-aged Yuppie in designer shorts and $300 shoes leaned down, wheezing. "What house?"

"The fortune-teller's house that was sitting right there." Nick pointed behind the jogger.

The guy backed away suspiciously. "There was no house there. I've been running this route every day for the past year, and that empty lot's always been an eyesore. You must be lost."

Yep, I'm lost all right, Nick decided, watching the man lope off. *I've taken advice from a psychic who doesn't exist. I've practically kept my wife prisoner for years with my obsessions. And then I almost kill an innocent kid. "Lost" about says it all.*

Then he thought of something else. How could he have a

real tattoo from an imaginary person?

Another mind picture immediately followed, and he frowned. *Gargoyle.* He had the cat Madame Nadine had given him; so, that must mean she existed. Right?

Nick closed his eyes and pressed his head on the steering wheel. The mother of all headaches pounded behind his eyes. He didn't understand any of this. Was Madame Nadine an angel or something? Had she been sent here to help him solve his problems? Or was it all a figment of his desperate imagination?

Nick knew his problems were about to get worse when he heard a motor behind him. He raised his head and looked in the rearview mirror.

A police car.

Great! Now everyone will know what a lunatic I've become.

The car door opened, and a female officer emerged.

His mouth dropped open, and his heart started beating like a jackhammer.

Paula, wearing a female police uniform, approached his open car window. Stern-faced, she asked, "What are you doin' here, fella? Admiring the view?" She jerked her head toward the sorry-looking lot.

"Looking for Madame Nadine."

Paula raised an eyebrow.

"She disappeared."

"Oh?"

"It appears she never existed."

That got her attention, but she quickly hid her interest. "It's illegal to loiter along a public highway, mister. I think I'm going to have to take you in."

"Listen, Paula, I'm not in the mood for games today. And you could get in big trouble impersonating an officer."

"You did it," she reminded him.

"I *am* an officer, dammit." Suddenly, he remembered and looked down at his watch. 2:00 P.M. His heart threatened to jump right out of his chest, and his blood began to roar in his ears. "Shouldn't you be somewhere about now?"

She ignored his question and strummed her fingertips on

the roof of the car.

He tried to ignore her puffy lips, swollen from his kisses, or the passion mark on her neck. More than anything in the world, he wanted to pull her into the car, on his lap, and tell her how much he missed her . . . *already.*

"I definitely think I'm going to have to take you in for questioning," she concluded. "Slide over."

"What?"

"Move over to the passenger side, mister. I'm confiscating this vehicle."

"Oh, Lord," he muttered, but inclined his head in compliance. He felt something hard brush his wrist and glanced down, his eyes widening with disbelief. She'd handcuffed his left hand to her right one. "Are you nuts?"

"Maybe." Then she had the nerve to wink at him. "I'm just making sure you don't escape this time."

"Escape? This time? Damn, Paula, would you watch where you're driving! You almost backended that car."

"I'm not used to driving with one hand manacled to a prisoner." She took the berm of the road at sixty miles per hour. Gravel was flying everywhere.

"I'm not your prisoner."

"Think again, buddy," she said, slanting him a seductive look, and yanked his chain.

"Ouch! That hurt."

She zigzagged in one lane and out another. Car horns blared. But she was smiling with unconcern. "Do you want me to turn on the radio?"

"No, I do not want you to turn on the radio," he gritted out. "Watch the damn road."

"Tsk-tsk." She took her hand off the steering wheel for a brief second and patted his handcuffed one. "Don't worry. I've got everything under control."

He closed his eyes, deciding it was better not to see. "Where are we going?"

She began to hum a soft tune, ignoring him.

He decided to ask the important question hammering away

in his head. "Why aren't you at the divorce hearing?"

She flashed him one of those woman looks. The one that said, "Men are so-o-o-o dumb."

He decided to go with the flow and relax.

His eyes swept her body, assessing her for the first time. In a deliberately lazy tone of voice, he said, "You look pretty good in a uniform."

"Yeah, I do, don't I?"

She looked sensational. The shirt hugged her breasts, outlining hard nipples, and the pants gave a clear, enticing view of hips and buttocks. He shook his head hard, mid-thought, and looked again. Yep, hard nipples and no panty line.

"You're not wearing any underwear," he accused her.

She winked . . . again.

He almost swallowed his teeth. Especially when she just missed sideswiping a car in the next lane.

Then, completely impervious to the honking cars and cursing drivers, she smiled at him. And he felt warm and suddenly full of hope.

"The uniform does look good, but not as good as that black lace thingee," he said, trying to disconcert her, the way she had him.

She blushed. "Teddy."

"Teddy who?"

"Not Teddy who. It was a black lace teddy."

"Oh."

"I went shopping today."

Big deal! My life's falling apart, and she goes to the mall.

"I bought you some new underwear . . . to replace those yellowed, shampooed ones."

"Oh." He tried to sound bored.

"I know you don't like bikini briefs, so I got boxers."

Boxers? Hmmm. That sounds safe. Boring, actually. "Thank you."

"In the daylight, they have NO imprinted all over them, but in the dark they glow fluorescently with YES, YES, YES—all over."

"Oh." Nick looked down and noticed a very unbored part

of his body. He hoped Paula didn't notice.

She did. And she winked . . . for the third time.

"And they're silk."

Uh-oh! What the hell was she up to? Before he had a chance to ask, Paula exited the highway into a residential area of Nutley. She drove confidently down one quiet, tree-lined street after another. He frowned in puzzlement. He couldn't remember anyone they knew in this neighborhood.

And, hey, she'd better stop interfering with his hero plan. It was hard enough playing a knight in shining armor without her tempting him to haul her up onto his horse and ride off into the sunset, or something.

Stopping before a small Cape Cod with a white picket fence, she killed the motor, staring straight ahead, suddenly grave.

"I took the VW back to the dealer this morning," she said suddenly, "and got my Volvo back."

"What?"

"I decided you were right."

Now, this is really interesting. Paula admitting I'm right about something.

"It isn't a safe car for the city. Besides, you didn't fit into it. And I want a car you can fit into."

He was afraid to ask what she meant. Instead, he focused on their present situation. Waving his free hand to indicate the quiet street, he asked, "Now what?"

She gulped nervously. "I want to show you something."

"I've already seen everything you've got to show."

"Tsk-tsk!"

"Of course, I wouldn't mind seeing it again."

"Behave, Nick. I'm serious. C'mon, let's get out." She opened her door and pulled him along beside her roughly.

"Hey, slow down. You're cutting off my circulation."

He thought she said something about wanting to cut off a lot more than his circulation.

They were standing in the front yard of the house. A FOR SALE sign standing in the grass and the curtainless windows announced its lack of occupants.

"How about undoing these cuffs? That guy looks like he's about to call the police."

Paula turned to see a man walking his dog, gaping at their handcuffed wrists. "I *am* the police," she muttered.

"Hah! And I'm Mickey Mouse."

"If you're Mickey, then I'm Minnie, babe."

"What's that supposed to mean?"

"Figure it out yourself, bonehead." She undid the lock and was about to pocket the cuffs.

"Yoo-hoo! Oh, yoo-hoo!"

He and Paula both turned toward the dog walker at the same time. He came closer, and Nick couldn't believe his eyes. The man sported gray hair spiked to a curly point on top, slacks pulled up to his armpits, and about four inches of white socks showing at the ankles. "Oh, my God, it's the guy from the bookstore."

"Really? The one who gave you the sex advice?" Paula asked.

"He did *not* give me sex advice," he corrected.

"And is that his wife, Lorna?" Paula said.

Just then, Nick noticed the short woman with the orange curls springing all over her head. She wore a mini skirt and halter top with sneakers and bobby socks. And she clung to the old man's arm, gazing at him adoringly, as if he were, yep, a knight in shining armor.

What is it with me and knights in shining armor today?

"Aren't they sweet," Paula cooed.

Nick looked at her as if she had a screw loose.

"Hey, good idea!" the old man yelled, pointing at the handcuffs. "Can Lorna and I borrow them later?"

"Oh, Fred, you rascal, you! You really are the bee's knees," Lorna simpered, batting her eyelashes flirtatiously at her husband.

"Durn tootin' I am." Fred-the-lech beamed.

Yep, I'm definitely going off the deep end. Any minute now, Madame Nadine will come flying by on her broomstick, or her cloud.

"So, did you get the lead back in your pencil?" the old coot asked with a chuckle.

Paula giggled, and Lorna nudged her husband with an elbow. Nick just put both hands on his hips and glared at Fred with consternation. "I never had trouble with lead in my pencil."

"Oh. My mistake. Guess you were lookin' for new ways to gas up the old engine. Heh, heh, heh. Took my advice, didja?"

If Fred weren't a senior citizen, Nick might have gone right over and belted him one. Paula latched on to his arm, just in case.

"Engines, huh?" Paula asked, "Did he recommend *that* book to you?"

Nick played dumb.

But Paula persisted, "You know, *How to Make Your Baby's Motor Hum When Her Engine Needs a Tune- Up*?"

He felt his face grow hot. "Oh, all right. Yes, he did," he snapped. "Now, can we drop it?"

Paula smiled and turned back to the couple. "Hey, Fred, not to worry! My motor's humming just fine now."

Nick made a strangled sound.

"We live next door," Lorna informed Paula conversationally. Nobody paid any attention to Nick; he could be choking to death for all they cared. "We're having a hot tub party next Saturday. Why dontcha come over, sweetie? And bring your hubby along."

Hubby? Nick choked even harder, unable to spit out the words, "Absolutely not!"

"Maybe," Paula said.

As the old couple walked off, waving, Nick turned back to Paula. Instead of laughing, as he'd expected, she was looking up at him in question, blinking nervously.

"Well, what do you think?" she said in a whispery voice.

"Of what? Those senior citizen sexpots? You being a police officer? Us being handcuffed? The weather?"

"The house?" she said in a small voice.

"The house?" That was the last thing he'd expected. He examined the building for the first time, and then, slowly, he began to understand. "Oh, Paula."

"Don't say no right off, Nick. I love this house. I've been looking at it for months," she said defensively. "I . . . I want to buy it."

His first reaction was to tell her to forget it. There was no security fence. The bay window in front would be an easy target for burglars. And Nutley was way too close to Newark and druggies out for quick money. But he saw the look of hope in her eyes, and he bit back his objections. "Well, let me see."

They began to walk around the house, and he stopped at his first glimpse of the backyard. *Oh, Lord!*

"What?" Paula exclaimed, seeing the look of horror on his face.

"Look! Look at that!" The whole back fence was lined with sunflowers. Hundreds of them. Bobbing in the sunlight. "Is this a joke?"

"What?"

"The sunflowers. You planted them here to play a joke on me, right?"

"I don't know what you're talking about. Nick, what's wrong? Why do you have tears in your eyes? Honey, don't. I can live without this house if you don't like it. It's just a house. We can move somewhere else."

"We?"

She tilted her head in confusion. "Of course, *we*. Did you think I would live here by myself?"

He wasn't sure what he thought. He could barely think for the pounding of his heart. "Paula, don't do this to me. Signing those papers this morning was the hardest thing I've ever had to do in my life. I did it because I love you, and—"

"I know."

"—I realize now that our divorce is for the best. I *am* obsessive. I have—what did you say? What do you mean, *you know*?"

She swung her right arm in a wide arc, like a windmill, and punched him in the stomach.

"Ooomph!" It didn't hurt much, but it sure surprised him.

"What the hell was that all about?"

"For leaving this morning without talking to me. Our biggest problem hasn't been your obsession with my safety, you big lunkhead. Or my carelessness. It's been your failure to communicate. And it's going to stop right now, babe." She jabbed a finger in his chest.

"It is?" He went still, hope unfurling in his chest like a giant balloon, choking off his air. He was afraid to believe what she seemed to be offering.

"Do you love me, Nick?"

"Of course."

"Ask me if I love you?"

"I don't have to ask. I know you love me, babe. That was never the iss—"

"Ask, dammit!"

"Do you love me, Paula?"

"More than life."

He said a quick prayer then and hoped that Madame Nadine would wing it on up to heaven, first class.

Paula took a step toward him.

He took a step toward her.

"Nick?"

"Paula?" He held open his arms, and she jumped into them, almost knocking him backward. Bracketing her face with his hands, he studied her face, his eyes probing to her very soul. "Are you coming back to me?" His voice shook with vulnerability, but he was too frightened to care.

She nodded, and he kissed her hungrily, holding her tight.

She was laughing and crying at the same time.

He was laughing and trying not to cry at the same time.

"God, I should be noble and walk away. I should love you enough to let you go. I should be a hero. I should—"

"Be quiet."

"Right!"

Tucking her into his side, he kissed her again quickly and began to walk toward the back door. "Maybe you'd better show me the inside of this place before we give the neighbors a show."

"Wouldn't this be a great place for all our cats?"

He groaned. He liked the sound of *our*, but then he exclaimed, "Cats! As in plural? No, Paula, uh-uh. Not in this lifetime. I mean, I've learned to compromise, but that's asking entirely too much. Cats! *Yech!*"

"Now, Nick, don't you think it would be kind of cute to name the kittens Sneezy and Grumpy and Dopey and—"

"Oh, great! Gargoyle and the Seven Dwarf-kits."

She offered him a sweet, arresting smile, and he groaned again.

As they entered the kitchen, he said, "Now give me those handcuffs."

"Why?" she asked, suddenly suspicious.

He looped his arms around her waist and grinned. "I just had another idea to satisfy your heart craving."

And right there, on the kitchen floor, he did just that.

Epilogue

Five years later
Happily ever after and then some . . .

Nick walked onto the back porch of his Nutley home, noting that the kitchen door was open and unlocked. He shrugged, having lost that argument long ago.

"Honey, I'm home," he called out, a smile in his voice. He couldn't help himself. Even after all these years, he felt such joy coming home to his wife.

Four heads popped up.

Paula's tummy was as big as the watermelon she was slicing on the new granite countertop installed last year when he had the kitchen remodeled for her. She smiled brightly at him in welcome. He knew without words that she felt the same joy on seeing him.

And his three little munchkins, two of whom, three-year-old twins Rita and Gloria, had been coloring at the kitchen table, yelled "Daddy!" and ran to be caught up in his arms, giving him sloppy little girl hugs and kisses. *Was there anything sweeter than the smell of little girl skin?* Nick wondered, *except maybe hot wife skin?* The third munchkin, one-year-old Anthony, sat in his high chair, flashing him a toothless grin, arms outstretched for Nick to pick him up.

Actually, it was six heads that popped up, for Gonzo and Gargoyle lay on their respective rugs on opposite sides of the kitchen. Gonzo, who was getting up in years, for a dog, lifted his head and gave a half-hearted *"Woof-woof,"* before returning his attention to the squeaky dragon toy he was guarding with his life. Gargoyle liked to steal the slimy fur thing and hide it when

Gonzo wasn't watching. Gargoyle turned to look at Nick, then resumed licking her fur as if to say, "Oh. It's just you!"

Nick put the girls down and walked over to link his arms around Paula's big bulk from behind. He kissed the side of her neck. "What's for dinner?" And nipped her neck, letting her know exactly what he was hungry for. Always.

"You're barbecuing," she said, arching her neck for another kiss. She pointed to the large number of hamburgers, hot dogs, ribs, and foil-wrapped potatoes sitting on the counter.

"What? We're feeding an army?" he grumbled.

"No. Just us. Skip and Lee with their latest girlfriends. Kahlita and her new husband. Fred and Lorna."

"That's all?" he grumbled.

"No," she said, turning to smile at him. A mischievous smile, if he ever did see one. "And our guest of honor." She was staring over his shoulder.

Okaay! He turned to see Richard Casale standing in the doorway leading to the den. He wore his new plebe uniform from the U.S. Naval Academy at Annapolis where he'd just started training two months ago.

"Richie!" He walked over, extending a hand to shake, then thought better of it and pulled him into a bear hug . . . one which Richie had no trouble returning, really hard.

Nick leaned back to get a better look at the boy with his newly shorn hair. He was so proud of the boy and the progress he'd made from the street thug he'd rescued five years ago. A straight A-student with fifteen hundred on his SATs! He and Paula had adopted Richie four years ago.

Later that evening, he sat in a chair on the porch, rocking a sleeping Tony in his lap. He watched his family and neighbors and friends as they mingled and chatted, the girls having long gone to their beds. His heart filled almost to overflowing, and tears filled his eyes at what he'd almost lost.

He chuckled then as he noticed the sunflowers that still flourished here, lining the back fence with heads the size of hubcaps. A constant reminder that everyone had heart cravings that needed to be fulfilled. Even him. Even when they didn't know what it was that they craved.

For him, it was love.

The End

Saving Savannah

A little lagniappe from Sandra to her fans.

A Note from Sandra Hill

Dear Readers:

Pull up a chair, pour yourself a tall glass of sweet tea, and listen to the musical sweetness of Beausoleil's "L'Ouragon" ("The Hurricane") while I stir the gumbo and tell you about the short story SAVING SAVANNAH. Would you care for a slice of Tante Lulu's famous Peachy Praline Cobbler Cake to go with your tea? No? How about another beignet? No? Well, maybe later.

SAVING SAVANNAH is yet another of Tante Lulu's adventures. When I first started writing these Cajun contemporaries about the wild LeDeux brothers, I never imagined how the old lady with a heart of gold would touch so many lives.

Although never in print before, SAVING SAVANNAH was offered free for a short time on my website. The Internet pirates soon put a stop to that idea. But now I've decided to update the story and expand it for all you fans of the outrageous Cajun traiteur and determined matchmaker, the favorite auntie we all wish we had.

Originally, SAVING SAVANNAH was meant to be a mini-prequel to my August 2009 romance, SO INTO YOU, the eighth novel in the Cajun series, but, really, it can stand on its own, out of order. In this story, you'll laugh and cry as the self-proclaimed Grandma Moses with an attitude bulldozes her way into the lives of Savannah Jones and her five-year-old daughter, Katie, who are homeless in post-Katrina New Orleans. It's hard to believe, isn't it, that people in Louisiana are still suffering from that devastating disaster, even after all these years? Thanks to Tante Lulu's newfound zest for helping the hurricane victims, not to mention her notorious matchmaking skills, ex-POW Captain Matthew Carrington discovers his former fiancée, mother of his child, working as a waitress in a strip joint. Sparks fly and humor abounds, guar-an-teed!

To learn more about my Cajun/Tante Lulu novels (THE LOVE POTION, TALL, DARK AND CAJUN, THE CAJUN COWBOY, THE RED HOT CAJUN, PINK JINX, PEARL JINX, WILD JINX and SO INTO YOU), visit my website at www.sandrahill.net or my Facebook page at Sandra Hill Author. Keep in mind, Tante Lulu is also featured in the novella JINX CHRISTMAS in the A DIXIE CHRISTMAS anthology, as well as in book three of the Deadly Angels series, KISS OF TEMPTATION. The old lady sure does get around!

Check out the Cajun recipe at the end of this story . . . a little lagniappe from Tante Lulu.

As always, I wish you smiles in your reading.

Sincerely,

Sandra Hill
New York Times and *USA Today* Bestselling Author

Chapter One

A lady's gotta do what a lady's gotta do . . .

"NO, I AM NOT taking you into a sex shop, *chère*."

"Why? It ain't as if I'm not old enough."

"No."

"Whatcha 'fraid of, Tee-John? Us modern ladies gotta keep up with the times. If men kin go ta these places, why cain't us wimmen?" Louise Rivard, best known as Tante Lulu, put her hands on her hips and glared up at her nephew John LeDeux, a Louisiana police detective.

"No."

"It's not like it's illegal or nothin'."

"No."

"Besides, it's called the Garden of Eden. It's prob'ly a religious sex shop."

Tee-John rolled his eyes and gave her another head-to-toe survey of disapproval. "Did you have to wear that hooker outfit?" He couldn't fool her. He was hoping to change the subject.

Not a chance! She smacked him on the arm with her St. Jude fly swatter. Truth to tell, if folks were staring their way, it was at Tee-John, who was once described by a TV reporter as "sex on a stick," whatever that meant. That George Clooney didn't have nothing on him. Or Richard Simmons, for that matter. Whoo-ee! That Richard Simmons could park his sneakers under her bed any day.

"*Thass* the tenth time you said that 'bout my 'pearance, and I doan appreciate yer sass any more'n I did the first time. Remember what I allus say. The gator doesn't see its own tail."

"Huh?"

"You should check out yer own tail before checkin' out mine."

"Never in a million years would I make an observation about yer tail, *chère*. I'm jist sayin' that maybe you ought to dress a little more, I don't know, dignified."

"Dignified, smignified!" she scoffed.

Because of her petite size, she did most of her shopping in the children's section of department stores, usually Walmart. "This is from the Hannah Montana collection, and Hannah Montana ain't no hooker."

"Hannah Montana has gotten older, and so have you. In fact, she's just Miley Cyrus now. You shoulda seen her at the video music awards show. Whoo-ee! On the other hand, ninety-two-year-old women should dress their age," he muttered.

She gave him a dirty look. "I might be so old I coulda made Fred Flintstone's bed rock, but I ain't dead yet."

Today she was wearing her Farrah Fawcett wig, a nod to the prettiest gal there ever was, an angel for real now, bless her heart. A glittery red tank top and tight white pedal pushers, or what they called capris today, were meant to accentuate her assets. But, truth to tell, she'd lost her boobs and butt about nineteen eighty-seven; as a result, she wore falsies, both above and below, to help Mother Nature. Wedgie, open-toed shoes with purple flowers completed her outfit. Her fingernails and toenails were painted Hot-To-Trot Red. To her mind, she looked darned good.

"I'm still not takin' you into a sex shop."

"You heard of Desperate Housewives, boy?" She still called him boy, even though he was close to thirty now. Compared to her, Moses was a boy. "How 'bout Desperate Nonagenarians?"

"Nona . . . what?"

"A person what's ninety-somethin'. I heard that word on that new cable TV show. *Sex After Seventy.*"

"You're makin' that up. Aren't you? Never mind! You about froze my brain with that picture. And I'm still not takin' you into a sex shop."

"Are you blushin'?" On tippy toes, she peered closer at her

nephew, once the baddest boy on the bayou before he married. Still was, truth to tell.

"Of course I'm blushin'. Is that why you wanted me to bring you to Nawleans t'day? Talk about!"

"No. I tol' you. I wanna go ta the Voodoo Palace. Not that I believe in voodoo, but the shop carries some herbs I ain't been able ta find anywhere else." Tante Lulu was a traiteur, or folk healer. Had been all her life, and a good one, if she did say so herself.

"It's at the end of this block." Tee-John grabbed her by the upper arm and practically frog-marched her down the street a ways.

"Stop pushin' me. I was jist kiddin' 'bout goin' in the sex shop, fer goodness sake." Then she noticed something interesting and stopped in her tracks. "Whass that?" That was the great thing about Nawleans. There was always something interesting going on.

Before them was a grungy-looking storefront with the windows blacked out. The sign read St. Christopher's House of Refuge.

"It's a homeless shelter or soup kitchen, or something," he said, attempting to tug her along.

She dug in her feet. St. Jude, patron of hopeless causes, was her favorite saint, but she'd like to know what St. Christopher was up to, as well. "Let's go in."

That's when Tante Lulu got a big shock. She'd lived in Southern Louisiana all her life. She knew the seedy side of the Big Easy. Even though her bayou region wasn't hit as hard as the city, she'd seen the news coverage of Hurricane Katrina and all its devastation.

What she hadn't known was that, years later, people were still suffering. Terribly. That just dilled her pickle. Was she really that insulated in her cozy bayou home? Bayou Black was only an hour away from the Crescent City, but apparently worlds away.

For the next hour she and Tee-John walked around the place, both of them shaking their heads with dismay. It was a huge room, like a warehouse, with a mural of New Orleans before the Civil War adorning the walls. She recalled then that this had been an opera house in the 1800s. There was a cafeteria-style meal service to the left where folks were lined up for breakfast, it being barely nine a.m. After filling their trays, they sat down at long folding tables.

At one end were a series of ladies' and men's rooms and showers for each of the sexes. Desks had been set up at the far side where social service people were advising folks on what benefits they could get—not much—and job opportunities—very little. Racks of used clothing and blankets occupied another area, along with giant bowls filled with hotel-sized personal products, like toothpaste, soap, and shampoo, probably donated by traveling businessmen.

She'd have to mention this to her niece Charmaine who owned a bunch of beauty salons. Charmaine, a self-proclaimed bimbo who was once Miss Louisiana before she married the hottest cowboy to put his tushie on a horse, probably had lots of this kind of stuff she could donate. Poor people didn't care if they were using last year's samples or a no-longer-popular scent like Peanut Butter Brickle.

"No kidding?" she'd asked Charmaine when she'd shown her a new manufacturer's display case last year highlighting ice cream scented shampoos, conditioners, body washes, and colognes.

"Oh, yeah," Charmaine had assured her. "Some ladies like to smell like ice cream flavors."

"I wonder if they attract lots of bees . . . or ants," Tante Lulu had wondered. What was wrong with good old Ivory soap anyhow?

Whatever! Ice cream scents were out this year, apparently, and tropical fruits were in. Go figure!

Most of the shelter space was filled with cots, hundreds of them, some of which were separated from their neighbors by hanging sheets. For families, Tante Lulu presumed.

The most pitiful thing was the belongings piled next to cots. Suitcases, boxes, big plastic trash bags filled with all their personal effects.

Tee-John explained that the Katrina floods wiped out certain neighborhoods, including ones with low-income housing. But instead of rebuilding the units, the government chose to sell the land to developers who were constructing more upscale dwellings way beyond the means of the poor people. "That on top of shutting down the HUD trailers," he added.

She wiped the tears welling in her eyes with her St. Jude handkerchief. It was then that she noticed one element all these people shared: hopelessness.

"The saints must weep over this travesty," she murmured.

Tee-John was staring at a curly-haired boy, no more than five, playing with two rusty old Matchbox cars. The little mite probably reminded him of his own son, Etienne. Distressed, he snarled at her, "Where's your famous St. Jude when he's needed so badly?"

She winced. It was hard sometimes to understand why God allowed certain things to happen.

"Do you wanna leave?" he asked, putting an arm around her shoulders.

She shook her head. "Not yet, but I need ta get some air."

When they were standing on the back porch, which faced a small parking lot, she straightened with determination. "We gotta do somethin' ta help."

"We who?" Tee-John inquired.

Knowing her nephew, Tante Lulu figured he would probably slip the little boy's mother a fifty-dollar bill. And he would mail a check to the shelter. She would, too.

But that was the easy way.

"Me and St. Jude, *thass* who, you idjet. St. Jude musta sent me here t'day. He's usin' me ta get a job done."

"Like an angel?" he teased.

"If *thass* what you wanna call me. All I know is God mus' wanna use me fer a higher purpose. A LeDeux family mission, I'm thinkin'."

Tee-John said, "I suspect you be callin' on me ta be one of yer 'missionaries'."

Living on Not-So-Easy Street . . .

SAVANNAH JONES was a master of deceit. She'd become so, by necessity, while living in the Big Easy these past few years.

It was just past dawn. On the road outside Butler Park in New Orleans, she was busy polishing her red Subaru, which she'd affectionately nicknamed Betty. It was fifteen years old, but it still ran, as long as she employed that special trick in getting the wonky ignition to start.

Park police usually made their first rounds by seven a.m. She would move her vehicle before then to another location, probably the Walmart parking lot. But, no, she'd used that two days ago, and the security guard was starting to eye her suspiciously. She could push her shopping cart inside only so many hours without buying anything. Maybe the Dunkin' Donuts. Or the parking lot behind St. Christopher's. Yes, that was it. The homeless shelter served breakfast on Tuesdays and wasn't so diligent about patrolling the premises. Plus, the authorities weren't as persistent about grilling folks at the meal area as they were at the sleeping quarters.

She gave Betty one last pat with her chamois. It was important that no one realize it was her home. Had been for three weeks now. Three weeks and two days. If she could survive for another two weeks, she would have enough money to move. Alaska or bust! That should be far enough away from . . . Never mind. She didn't need to start her day on a negative note.

"Did you get the tree sap off, honey?" she asked the little girl who was studiously rubbing the fender beside her. At five, Katie was the sweetest little thing, not at all difficult.

"Yep. An' some bird poop, too." She smiled up at her, showing the empty spaces in her mouth where she was missing two front teeth. "I'm hungry, Mommy."

"I know, sweetie. We'll have breakfast soon. After we go to the Y. Then I'll drop you off at kindergarten."

"I don't wanna go t'day," Katie whined.

"You have to, darling. You know that. Mommy has to go to work."

"Why can't I come with you?"

Oh, yeah, that would work. Crazy Hal of Crazy Hal's Strippers and Dippers would just love having her wait tables with a kid tagging along at her side. Hal's was famous for its boneless hot wings with twelve different dipping sauces, but even more famous for the twenty-four-hour-a-day strippers. It was no environment for a child.

"You just can't, sweetie. But we'll do something special tonight. Maybe go to a movie." It was dollar night, kids free, at the Bijou on Tuesdays. "Okay?"

"Okay. Kin we have popcorn . . . with butter?"

"Sure thing, short stuff." She ruffled Katie's black corkscrew curls, which were unlike her long, straight blond hair but just like Katie's father's. Father and daughter also shared the same mischievous dark caramel eyes. Her were a darkish blue. Immediately, Savannah crushed the image. It hurt too much and served no purpose. Matt was gone and never coming back, one of the multitude of soldiers lost in Afghanistan.

Katie yawned widely, setting down her rag.

It broke Savannah's heart to see her daughter living this way. Heck, it broke her heart to see herself living this way. When she graduated from the University of Georgia eight years ago with high honors in secondary education, she never would have guessed that she would be jobless and homeless one day. In fact, when she'd had Katie five . . . almost six years ago, she'd been teaching full-time and was living in a nice apartment.

Savannah hated self-pity, but, honestly, she had become the poster girl for Murphy's Law. Whatever could go wrong, did, in her unfortunate case.

It started with Hurricane Katrina. Her apartment and almost all of her belongings were swept away in the flood. Then the school where she was a teacher closed, and all the children were parceled out to other districts. The school never reopened. Despite her excellent credentials, she was unable to find another permanent teaching job locally.

Until recently, she was able to get by with substitute teaching, but because of government cutbacks, those assignments dried up.

In order to move to Alaska, where she heard employment opportunities abounded, she figured she needed five thousand dollars. Thus far, she had only three thousand. Murphy's Law again, what with a mugging and a long bout with the flu, not to mention the dentist and pediatrician for Katie. Two steps forward and one step back.

Living in her car ended up being her only option for saving, unless she wanted to risk losing her daughter by going into a homeless shelter. Child Protective Services hovered there, like vultures. Oh, she had to give CPS credit. They did good for lots of neglected or abused kids, but they also thought nothing of taking a child away from her mother. Being homeless and working in a strip joint did not stack in her favor.

By the time she and Katie had completed their early morning swim at the Y, followed by a quick shower and change of clothes, they were both starving. Luckily, the St. Christopher shelter was still serving breakfast.

When they'd gone through the line and were about to sit down, Savannah noticed an old lady staring at her. A really strange old lady. Wearing tight capri pants with a glittery red tank top, a huge blond wig disproportionate to her small stature, and a generous slathering of make-up. Actually, she resembled a dolled-up version of that actress Estelle Getty who used to be on the TV show *Golden Girls*.

More important, Savannah was pretty sure the same woman had been watching her when she pulled into the parking lot a short time ago. Not a good thing. Hers and Katie's clothing were stacked to the roof of the back seat, along with clear plastic boxes holding all their belongings, including photo albums she had luckily rescued before the flood. A person wouldn't have to be a rocket scientist to figure out their situation. Staying under the radar had been Savannah's code for too long to not be fearful of any attention now.

She led Katie to the back of the room, far from the serving

area where the woman continued to stare suspiciously at her. With their backs to the cafeteria, she and Katie sat down and dug in. Scrambled eggs and toast. Pancakes and syrup. Oatmeal and dry cereal. All washed down with milk for Katie and black coffee for her. She would take several packets of crackers and a carton of orange juice with her for later.

"Hello."

Savannah jumped with surprise, almost knocking over her coffee. Katie giggled at her side.

The old lady sank down into a chair across from them. No more than five feet tall, she had to lift her arms to rest her elbows on the table.

"Are you a grandma?" never-bashful Katie blurted out. "I don't have no grandma." The little devil pouted her lips with exaggerated woe. Her daughter had been on a grandmother kick for a week, ever since the grandmother of a classmate brought chocolate cupcakes to school. So far no questions about a daddy, thank God.

"No, but I'm an auntie. My real name is Louise Rivard, but you kin call me Tante Lulu. *Thass* what everyone calls me. Tante means aunt."

Katie's eyes went wide. She tried the words out hesitantly. "Tan-te. Lu-lu. You talk funny."

"Katie!" Savannah admonished.

Katie ignored her and continued talking to the stranger. "Are you Spanish? My teacher, Miss Sanchez, is from Party Rico."

Tante Lulu laughed. "No, *mon petit chou*, I'm jist Cajun from down the bayou."

Savannah had thought she detected that lyrical accent prevalent in Southern Louisiana. Having an English minor in college, she'd once done a paper on the various patois prevalent throughout the South. The Cajun dialect was by far the most fascinating.

But wait. Her persistent daughter had a new idea, and before Savannah could halt her running tongue, the little girl asked with wonder, "You'll be my aunt, too?"

Whoa, whoa, whoa! Too much, too soon. Not ever.

"Sure. Jist like I am to my nieces and nephews, Luc, Remy, René, Tee-John and Charmaine, and ta all the folks that ain't blood kin but like family anyways."

Katie practically beamed.

Savannah bristled.

"And who 'zackly are you, sweetheart?" The wily old witch was addressing her daughter, probably sensing that she would get no response from the mother.

"Katherine Mary Carrington."

Savannah was going to have a talk with Katie again, the one where she insisted on caution with strangers, even seemingly innocent looking old ladies.

"What a pretty name fer such a pretty little girl!"

Katie preened. "But you kin call me Katie, like my mommy does."

"Even prettier," the old lady remarked, then looked pointedly at Savannah.

Realizing that there was no avoiding the woman, she said, "Savannah Jones."

"I ain't never heard of anyone named Savannah. It could be worse. I had a third cousin named Galveston. Tee, hee, hee!"

At least she hadn't commented on her and Katie's different last names. Although she'd never married Katie's father, Matt Carrington, she'd given her baby his surname at birth. Big mistake, she'd learned later. Matt's parents would love to take their only grandchild away from Savannah, and her being homeless would give them all the ammunition they'd need. Thus the need for anonymity and caution.

"I was born in Savannah," she explained. Not that she had any reason to defend a perfectly good name.

"I dint mean no offense," the old lady said with genuine regret.

Just then a tall, good-looking guy in khakis, a black T-shirt, and a blazer sat down next to the old lady and smiled at her and Katie. He carried two styrofoam cups of coffee, one of which he placed in front of Tante Lulu.

"This is my nephew John LeDeux. We call him Tee-John." To Katie, she explained, "That means Little John 'cause when he was a boy, he was the littlest LeDeux."

The guy grinned and winked at Katie. He better not wink at Savannah. She was immune to good looking men who promised the moon and then . . . *Oh, God! Why do I keep thinking about Matt today? I've got to focus, and besides, this guy is wearing a wedding band.* Not that marriage inhibited some jerks. Working where she did brought that fact home every day.

Katie flashed a toothless smile and said, "Maybe I could be Tee-Kate."

"Sure as gators got snouts." Tante Lulu smiled back, then added to Savannah, "Tee-John is a cop up Fontaine way."

Savannah stiffened. *Okaaay! Time to get this show on the road!* She began to gather up the remains of their breakfast. "We have to go," she whispered to Katie.

The old lady and the man exchanged glances.

Her reaction had caused them to be suspicious, Savannah could tell, but she couldn't help herself. Every time she saw a policeman come in her direction, she figured that Matt's parents or CPS had finally found her and were about to take Katie away. For all she knew, that's exactly who this one was, though she didn't think a hired cop would bring his elderly aunt along.

"What's yer rush?" the nosy old biddy asked.

"I have to take Katie to kindergarten." She checked the wall clock. "We only have fifteen minutes."

"And Mommy has to go to work so we can earn enough money to go to Alaska. There's polar bears in Alaska. And seals. We looked on the computer at the library."

Savannah groaned inwardly at her daughter's running tongue.

"And where do you work, honey?" the old lady asked Savannah.

Before she could come up with some hazy answer and drag her daughter away, Katie revealed with a giggle, "Crazy Hal's."

What was it with the giggling today? Katie had become a regular giggle machine. "Isn't that a crazy name?"

"Sure is, sweetie," Tante Lulu agreed.

But the guy gave Savannah a knowing look. Obviously, he was familiar with Crazy Hal's.

"I'm a waitress, not a stripper." *Not that it's any of your business.*

"Strippers are ladies that take off all their clothes," her precocious daughter whispered to Tante Lulu.

The guy pulled a deck of cards out of his pocket. "Do you like magic tricks, Katie? I always carry these in my pocket because I have a little boy your age who loves card tricks."

Katie nodded enthusiastically.

He began to deal them both cards and explain some game to Katie in a low voice. It soon became obvious why. He was giving his aunt time to get Savannah in her crosshairs.

"Girl . . ." Tante Lulu started to say.

At first, Savannah didn't realize she was talking to her. At twenty-nine, she couldn't remember the last time anyone had referred to her that way. And sometimes she felt so tired, she could be ninety-nine.

"Are you in trouble?" Tante Lulu continued.

"What? Why would you ask that?"

"Because St. Jude, he's tappin' on my shoulder ta beat the band."

She'd always wanted to be a private dick . . .

"DID YOU GET her license number?" Tante Lulu asked Tee-John as the red Subaru peeled out of the parking lot.

"Yep."

"What kin you find out about her?"

"Pretty much everything."

"Her address?"

"Usually, except I'm thinkin' she lives in that car."

Tante Lulu gasped. "Why wouldja say that?"

"All the signs are there. Looks like everything they own is in that car. Bed rolls and pillows. Labeled plastic boxes. Toiletries. Clothes. Shoes. Toys. Stuff like that."

"Thass awful. If she has a waitress job, why wouldn't she

have a place ta live, even if it ain't real nice? And if she's short of cash ta pay fer an apartment, why wouldn't she stay at the homeless shelter?"

"She's probably afraid of losing her daughter. Plus, I'd bet my left nut—I mean, my left arm that's she's on the run."

"From what?"

"Don't know, but I'll find out. Guar-an-teed."

"I gave her my bizness card, in case she's in trouble."

"You have a business card?"

"'Course, I do. I need it fer my traiteur bizness. It has the St. Jude prayer printed on the back."

"That should help Savannah."

He probably didn't know that she could recognize sarcasm when it hit her in the face. What an idjet! "Yer darn tootin' it will."

Then she said a little prayer in her head. *We got us a mission, Jude.* At least, she thought she'd said it in her head.

But then, Tee-John said, "Jist don't be draggin' me inta any more of your acts of mercy. Last time I ended up bailin' you out of the slammer."

"I dint ask you ta help. In fact, I was havin' fun. You meet all kinds of interestin' folks in jail, y'know?"

John's jaw dropped, as it often did when in the company of his wacky great-aunt. *I know! I'm a cop. I deal with those "interestin'" folks every day.*

"The food ain't so good, though. I tol' the captain he needs ta find a cook what knows how to make a good roux. The gumbo was downright disgustin'."

Rolling his eyes, John cautioned, "You need to slow down, auntie. Relax and enjoy yer golden years!" *Like that is ever gonna happen.* Even so, Tante Lulu was getting old, and he hated the idea of her overdoing and ending up in a hospital or worse. She was precious to him and all his family, despite her interfering, outrageous ways. Probably because of those interfering, outrageous ways.

"Pfff! There ain't nuthin' golden about creakin' bones and farts what slip out without warnin'."

He chuckled before he had a chance to catch himself.

"Besides, I like helpin' people."

"Even when they don't want yer help?"

"Specially when they doan want my help. Those are the ones needin' me most. Wait, wait, wait. Doan be in such a rush."

What now? He was steering her toward their parked car in hopes of getting out of Nawleans before noontime.

"I tol' you I need ta go to the Voodoo Palace over on Dumaine Street."

He'd been hoping she would forget. As he drove them over, he asked, "What herbs are you missing? I thought you had every weed and plant that ever grew." The pantry off the kitchen of her bayou cottage was overflowing with hanging dried plants and shelves of all her different herbs in labeled bottles along with ancient ledgers spelling out her remedies. As a child, he'd loved standing in there, sniffing the various intriguing scents.

"A love potion."

"Huh?" His mind must have been wandering. Did she really say . . . ? "Um, you have someone who's looking for a love potion?"

"Heck, no! I'm wantin' some fer myself. Have you seen that new butcher over at Boudreaux's General Store?"

He had to think for a minute. Then, he exclaimed, "Tante Lulu! Thass Boudreaux's great-grandfather, Gustave, helpin' out over the summer. He's almost bald and walks with a cane."

"Yeah, but have you checked out Gus's hiney?"

Un-be-liev-able! "Can't say that I have."

"Watch yer sass, boy. Even us older ladies notice a man's back side now and then. Ain't nuthin' wrong with that."

"His hiney, huh? Does Gus have a fart problem, too?"

She smacked him on the arm. "If you weren't so busy bein' sarcastic, you would have noticed the man's cute hind end." She waved a Richard Simmons fan in front of her face to emphasize her point.

What could he say to that? "And you need a love potion because . . . ?"

"Because Gus pays me no nevermind. Even when I wear

my 'Wild Girl' T-shirt, he doan even blink my way."

"Why don't you just get some of Sylvie's hopped up jelly beans?"

Years ago, his half-brother Luc's wife, Sylvie, who was a chemist, invented a love potion that she put in jelly beans. What a stink there was in the newspapers about that! The product never was sold to the public.

"First of all, Luc gave Sylvie strict orders not ta give me any. I cain't imagine why."

John could. Being an inveterate matchmaker, Tante Lulu would probably be feeding them indiscriminately to every couple she deemed worthy, whether they wanted them or not. Like the time she planned a secret wedding for his half-brother René and his nemesis, a court TV lawyer. The wedding had been a secret to everyone, including the bride and groom.

"Secondly, Sylvie claims they doan really work."

"Seemed to work with Luc. He was head over heels in love with her after popping a few of the candies."

"Thass what I said."

"Has it ever occurred to you that Gus has cataracts? Boudreax tol' me when I picked up that poke of okra fer you. His PawPaw is goin' in fer surgery soon. His vision's so bad that he gave Millie Pitot ham hocks when she asked fer chicken thighs last week."

"So, it wasn't me?" Tante Lulu smiled. "Well, I want some of those love potion herbs anyways. You never know when I might need ta do some emergency matchmakin'."

Emergency matchmaking? He didn't want to think what that might mean.

"Mebbe that Savannah gal needs a little help in the love department."

Yeah, a homeless stripper living in a car with her five-year-old kid is thinking of a man. More like where her next meal is coming from. That's what he thought, but what he said was, "Whatever you say, auntie."

Chapter Two

Georgia . . . and other things . . . on his mind . . .

CAPTAIN MATTHEW Carrington, U.S. Army Special Forces, sat down at a desk in the temporary office assigned to him at Fort Dix in New Jersey. He was so shocked, he felt gut-shot.

After five years of hell in an Al-Qaeda prison, after torture that would haunt him for life, after a badly tended leg wound that gave him a limp, and after six months of multiple surgeries and rehab in a D.C. hospital, he'd thought he couldn't be hurt any more. He was wrong.

He examined the creased and stained envelope in his shaking hands. It had so many forwarding addresses, it was amazing that it had actually caught up with him. From Georgia to three different Army Post Offices to five other addresses, it had traveled, finally sitting in a dead mail box until some postal employee had given it one more shot.

He pulled the letter out and read it once again. It was dated more than five years ago.

Dear Matt:

You've been gone for a week now, and I haven't heard from you. I know, I know, you hate letter writing, and you're probably still in transit. You need to give me your new email address, BTW. Your old one isn't working.

First of all, I love my ring. I'm looking at it now and getting tears in my eyes. I swear it is the most beautiful engagement ring a woman has ever received.

There's something I need to tell you, honey. Pretend

you hear a drum roll. I just can't wait any longer.

I'm pregnant.

I know, I should have told you in person, but I didn't want to ruin our time together. You said, repeatedly, that we'd set a wedding date when you came home, and we'd have kids sometime in the future. The future is now, sweetheart.

It happened, and there's nothing I can do about it. Actually, I'm ecstatic. Our baby might be unplanned, but it will be more than welcome. By me, anyhow. Please, please, please tell me that you're happy, too.

Gotta go now. I'm writing over my lunch break, and my one o'clock Creative Fiction class is waiting. I'll write again tomorrow. I just wanted to get this in the mail ASAP.

Love you forever,
Savannah

He could kick himself for not setting up a new email account as soon as he hit Afghanistan, but he hadn't had time. He'd been immediately engaged in briefings for an upcoming mission, which turned out to be his gateway to hell.

Ever since he'd come back to the States a month ago, he'd been trying to contact Savannah, but she seemed to have disappeared off the face of the earth. All his mail had been returned Forwarding Order Expired, including the dozens of letters he'd written from the hospital. He couldn't find a phone number for her or a trace of her current whereabouts on the Internet. Finally, he'd given up, figuring she'd delivered to him the GI's dreaded silent shaft. It wasn't her style, but maybe she'd met someone else and didn't have the nerve to tell him in person. Shit happened.

And now, just as he was about to go on leave, his commanding officer had handed him this letter. Straightening with determination, he picked up the phone and dialed a certain number.

"Mom?"

"Matt! Darlin'!" His mother's deep Southern drawl was warm with welcome. "When will you be getting here? Your father's at the club. He'll be so disappointed to have missed your call."

His parents had visited several times while he was at Walter Reed Medical Center, but this would be his first trip back home.

"I'll still arrive about seven p.m., but, Mom, I have a question for you. When you came to the hospital, I asked if you knew where Savannah was, and you said no."

There was an ominous silence before she said, "That is still true." She laughed, a fake laugh, if he ever heard one. "I don't know why you're still interested in that girl. Good Lord, she didn't even know her parents. She had no birth name. She was abandoned. An orphan! I shudder to think what might be in her genes. I always said you were too good for—"

"Enough! I didn't like you talking Savannah down before, and I don't like it now." He shook his head with disgust. Something was fishy here. *Slow down and think*, he told himself. *Sometimes a soldier needs to regroup and try a different tactic.* "Mother, did Savannah ever contact you or Dad after I was deployed almost six years ago?"

The silence was telling.

"Did you know she was pregnant?"

Her gasp carried through the telephone line. He could just picture her with a hand held delicately to her heart. "Yes, but—"

He said a foul word that he'd never said in his mother's presence before. "Did you see the baby?"

"Yes, but—"

"Boy or girl?"

"A girl. Her name is Katherine Mary Carrington. I told Savannah she had no right to give the baby our name, but she probably used it as a ploy to gain money from us."

A little girl. Oh, God! I have a daughter. And she would be . . . five years old already. Oh, God!

"Did you give her money?"

"Of course not!"

"Did she ask for money?"

"Well, no, not exactly, but—"

For Savannah to go to his parents for anything, knowing how his mother felt about her, there must have been some emergency. "She was my fiancée. Why would you refuse to help her with anything?"

"She could have hocked that too-expensive engagement ring you bought her if she had that many troubles."

"And did you tell her so?" he asked with brutal calm.

"I did, indeed. The hussy had the nerve to turn around and walk away. Good riddance to bad rubbish, if you ask me."

Matt saw red. He literally understood for the first time in his life what people meant when they used that hackneyed expression. Through the haze of fire floating in front of his vision, he gritted his teeth, knowing he needed more information before he could end the call. "Are they still in Savannah?"

"No. At least I don't think so."

"Savannah must have given up her teaching job. I called the school, and all they would tell me was that she was no longer employed there and hadn't been for years. She loved her teaching job. They wouldn't have fired her for a pregnancy; that's against the law. Do you know why she left?"

"Um . . . I have no idea. I mean, we offered to . . . well, never mind."

"You offered *what*?"

"We offered to bring up the girl, if you must know, once we were told of the birth by a friend of ours at the hospital. Doctor Morgan. You remember him, don't you? His daughter Emily used to play tennis with you at the club."

"About the baby?" he prodded.

"Oh. Well, all Savannah had to do was sign the papers, but she tore them up and threw them at us. Can you imagine?"

"You saw her then? The baby?"

"Briefly. She looked like you did as an infant, actually. And at that point, as far as we knew, you were probably dead. It would have been our last link with you. Our only child!" She barely stifled a sob.

Matt was not touched with sympathy for his mother. He knew from experience that she could sob at will when it suited her purposes. And he noticed that she'd referred to her granddaughter as "it." Some life that child would have had under his mother's care.

"You must admit, Matthew, we have much more to offer than a single mother," his mother continued, apparently recovered from her brief bout of grief, "but Savannah wouldn't listen. In fact, she had the gall to have a security officer escort us from the hospital."

Good for her! "Why didn't you tell me as soon as you realized I was alive?"

"We didn't want to worry you. Especially not in the beginning, when you were in the hospital recovering from physical injuries."

"And later, when I asked where Savannah was?"

"We didn't lie. We don't know where she is. We even had a court date, several, in fact, and she never showed up."

"A court date for what? No, don't tell me. A custody hearing. No wonder she disappeared."

He'd always known his parents were snobs of the highest order, but he'd mostly been amused by their exaggerated sense of self-importance. He'd never thought they could be so deliberately cruel.

"Did you threaten Savannah?"

"Of course not. We just offered to take it off her hands."

"It? It? Are you referring to my daughter . . . to your grandchild . . . as an 'it'? Thus far, I've heard you call her 'the girl,' 'the baby,' and 'it.' Don't you have a friggin' heart?" He was shouting now. He couldn't help himself.

"Matthew David Carrington! Don't you dare take that tone with—"

For the first time in his life, he hung up on his mother, and he pulled the plug on the land phone when it immediately started ringing.

Two hours later, he was on a flight to Georgia. In the past, when he was happily on his way home after a long mission, that Gladys Knight song "Midnight Train to Georgia" would play in his head. This time, he for damn sure wasn't happy. He pulled his wallet out of his back pocket and looked, for about the thousandth time, at the photo of himself and Savannah taken two weeks before his deployment, on the night he'd asked her to marry him. They looked so happy.

Was she happy now?

Had she built a new life for herself without him?

Where the hell did she think he'd been all this time? He'd forgotten to ask his mother. Probably dead. Yep, he'd bet his stripes that his mother would have told her he was deceased, not MIA.

Another unwelcome thought came to him. What if she'd married and his little girl was calling another man daddy?

"Oh, Savannah, where are you?" he whispered, pressing the picture to his lips. Tears welled in his eyes, but then he raised his head with determination. "I'm on my way, sweetheart, wherever you are."

Some puzzles just take time to solve . . .

"I JIST CAIN'T understand why she won't accept my help. I've asked her ta come stay here with me," Tante Lulu told Tee-John as they sat in rockers on her Bayou Black back porch. Tee-John's five-year-old son Etienne was down at the bayou stream fishing. Or more accurately, scaring away every fish, bird, and small animal within fifty feet with his wild casting technique.

Tee-John took a draw on his long neck bottle of beer, then wiped his mouth with the back of his hand, even though there was a perfectly good St. Jude napkin sitting on the wicker table beside him.

"She's afraid, Tante."

"Of what?"

"I'm not sure."

She gave him a narrow-eyed look, the one that had been

working since he was a young'en causing mischief up and down the bayou. "How kin you not be sure?"

"I'm a detective, not a magician. Besides, I've been stickin' close ta home with Celine bein' pregnant and all." She was in the house at the moment, taking a nap on the same cot Tee-John slept on all those years ago when he ran away from his father, Valcour LeDeux, when he got to drinking. That man was meaner than a grizzly with a corncob up its butt.

Imagine. Tee-John having another chile. And this time he would be around to see the *bebe* be born. "I hope she has a girl this time."

"That would be nice, but Etienne sez it better be a boy or we're sending it back."

She had to smile at that. The little imp! "Back ta Savannah. Fer two weeks, I been goin' over ta Nawleans ta talk with her. You were right, she's livin' in her car. I ain't et so many chicken dippers in all my life. I think I'm startin' ta cluck."

"Oh, Lord! You've been going to that strip joint, haven't you?"

"Yeah, and I'm learnin' some good dance moves, too. Didja ever hear of the twerk?"

"I'm afraid to ask."

"It involves bendin' yer knees and spreadin' them. Sorta like squatin' ta pee in the woods."

"I pee against a tree."

She swatted him on the knee with her folded Richard Simmons fan for the interruption. "Then you vibrate yer tushie real fast. You could say it's like shimmyin' yer butt. Me and Charmaine been practicin'. When Charmaine showed Rusty how it was done, he almos' had a heart attack. Then he took her ta bed fer a whole afternoon. Leastways, thass what Charmaine said. Want me ta demonstrate?"

"Please don't." He was staring at her like she was a little bit crazy. Nothing new there. "I bet Savannah is pissed about you bird-doggin' her."

"You could say that. Las' night, fer example, I followed her around Walmart 'til she stopped and asked what I was doin' there. I tol' her there ain't no law sez I cain't shop wherever I want. 'At midnight?' she asked then. Jeesh! I did buy her little girl a pretty sundress, though."

"I'm afraid to ask how you got ta Walmart, presumably in Nawleans, at that ungodly hour. No. Don't tell me. I'll be the one havin' a heart attack then. I'm surprised that Savannah accepted your gift."

"She couldn't not accept. I tore off the tags and ripped up the sales receipt." She thought for a few moments. "Mebbe we should kidnap the two of 'em."

"We are not kidnapping anyone. Get that idea out of yer head right now."

"You doan have ta yell."

"Sometimes yellin' is the only thing that will get through yer fool head."

"You ain't helpin' much."

Tee-John shrugged. "I gave you all the info I could find."

"Tell me again."

"Savannah Jones, born almost thirty years ago at St. Margaret's Hospital in Savannah, Georgia. No known birth parents. Adoptive parents, James and Ellie Jones, deceased. A graduate of the University of Georgia with high honors. Had been an English teacher at a private school in suburban Savannah. Then suddenly, she resigned and moved to Nawleans where she taught school in the lower ninth ward until Hurricane Katrina. She lost her apartment and her job because of the floods and hasn't been able to get back on her feet since then."

"There's a puzzle in there somewheres. I jist ain't figgered out what it is yet."

"Oh, I forgot ta tell you. A friend of mine in Georgia dug up something interestin'. Turns out Savannah got engaged to a Captain Matthew Carrington, just before he shipped out for Afghanistan more than five years ago. Todd and Evelyn Carrington, his parents, are big-shot, country-club types. Carrington was a POW for several years, but he escaped about six months ago. That's all I know."

Tante Lulu smacked him on the arm. "You knew that and

dint tell me. Sometimes, I swear, you got the brain of a flea."

"I was gonna tell you."

"Hah! I doan suppose you got any addresses or telephone numbers."

He pulled an index card out of his shirt pocket and grinned at her.

She grinned back.

"Be careful what you do, auntie. Savannah is runnin' from somethin', and it could very well be this guy. Maybe he was abusive. Or maybe he didn't care about being a father or a husband."

"I'll be careful. Jist you watch me. I know how ta handle people. I'm a people person."

Tee-John rolled his eyes.

She didn't care if he was skeptical. Tante Lulu had a feeling she was about to solve the puzzle. *Thank you, St. Jude.*

Chapter Three

A good soldier needs a battle plan . . .

MATT WAS AT HIS parents' home packing up the rest of his belongings to ship to his Fort Dix apartment. In the meantime, he was staying at a hotel. No way was he going to live at home, not after what his parents had done.

He was now on leave, and he was meeting this afternoon with a private detective who had a good track record for finding missing persons.

The phone rang as he was carrying the last of his boxes through the hall and down the steps. He heard his mother answer in the library.

"Yes, this is the home of Matthew Carrington. Who is this?"

Glancing in the open doorway, he saw his mother bristle. "I am Evelyn Carrington, if you must know. Why do you wish to speak with my son? Don't you dare call me an old biddy . . . you . . . you old biddy. I'm going to hang up now."

That's all he needed, his mother screening his calls. Matt put down his box and stepped in the room, signaling his mother to hand him the phone.

"Hello. Matthew Carrington here."

"Thank the Lord!" an elderly sounding voice with a Southern accent exclaimed. "I'm Louise Rivard, but you kin call me Tante Lulu, like everyone does. Are you the Matthew Carrington that was engaged to Savannah Jones?"

The fine hairs stood out on the back of Matt's neck, and he felt as if a vice were clamping his heart. He sank down into the desk chair. "Yes," he replied hesitantly.

"Boy, you are harder to find than pepper in a pile of pig poop."

Is she calling me the pepper or the poop? "Boy? I'm thirty-five years old."

"So? I usta play jacks with Moses. What does age have ta do with this?"

The woman is obviously a wack job. "Yes, I was engaged to Savannah. Do you know where she is?"

"Sure do."

The vice around his heart lessened, and he breathed deeply. "Is she okay?"

"No, she's not okay. Would I be callin' you if she was okay? Jeesh! Some men are dumber 'n a flyin' brick."

The damn vice slammed shut again. "What's wrong?"

"Wrong? I'll tell you what's wrong. She's poor as a bayou church mouse, workin' in a strip joint, and about ta skedaddle off ta live in an igloo or sumpin'."

Huh? "And my daughter . . . is she with her?"

"I declare, the Taliban musta done that water drip torture on yer brain, bless yer heart. And by the way, I 'preciate yer service to our country. I give ta the Wounded Warrior Project all the time."

"My daughter . . . ?" he prodded.

"Of course Katie is with her mother. Ain't you been listenin'?"

Katie. Her nickname is Katie. Something else occurred to him then. Savannah is a stripper. He found that hard to believe. They'd made love in the dark, at first, because she was too shy to let him see her naked. "Savannah is actually working in a strip joint?"

The old lady let out a snort of laughter. "Guess you'll hafta come and find out." Then she added, "I find it interestin' that yer more concerned about her job than the fact she and yer daughter are homeless, living in an ol' rattletrap of a car."

Matt put his face down on the desk and groaned inwardly. This just got worse and worse. "Give me her address, and I'll be there in . . . wait a minute. Where are you calling from?"

"Loo-zee-anna."

He grinned, suddenly giddy with relief and anticipation. "That's a big state. Where exactly are Savannah and Katie?"

"Well, thass the thing. I cain't tell you 'til I'm sure it's safe."

He stiffened. "What do you mean? Is she with someone else? Did she get married?"

"Savannah's still single, but she's skittish as a long-tailed cat in a room full of rockin' chairs. That girl's been on the run fer some time. How do I know it's not you she's runnin' from?"

He swore a blue streak and demanded, "Where the hell is she?"

"You ain't gonna accomplish nothin' with cuss words."

"Sorry," he said, realizing he couldn't afford to antagonize his only lead to date. "What do you want me to do?"

"Come meet with me so I kin check you out."

He resented the idea. Big time. Still he said, "Where?"

"Bayou Black. Thass outside Houma, Loozeanna. Jist ask anyone fer Tante Lulu's place."

"I'll be there." He checked his watch, saw that it was already seven p.m., and added, "Tomorrow morning."

"Okey-dokey. One last thing. Savannah thinks yer dead."

This just keeps getting worse and worse. "What? I was a prisoner of war, never officially declared dead."

"That ain't what yer mother tol' her."

He was about to confront his mother, but decided that could wait.

"Do you have one of them dress uniforms . . . like that Richard Gere wore in *An Officer and a Gentleman*? Wimmen drool over stuff like that."

Yeah, that's what I want. Grandma Moses getting the hots for me. Not! "I have a dress uniform," he offered hesitantly, "but Gere played a Navy officer, I think, and I'm Army. Army Special forces."

"Thass even better. We Cajuns like ta do things up right when it comes ta grand reunions. The Cajun Village People, a surprise weddin', that kinda thing."

"Huh?"

"You gotta play this jist right, *cher*. Knock Savannah's socks off . . . or her panties, as my nephew Tee-John would say. Tee-hee-hee!"

Am I really about to take love advice from a senior citizen?

"Wimmen melt over men in uniform."

That he did know for true. Yo-yo panties were not uncommon for soldiers picking up chicks in a singles bar, especially near a base just before deployment.

"I remember the time my Phillipe came home from the war jist before D-Day." Her sigh could be heard over the telephone lines.

This woman is hundred-proof crazy. Still, she was his only link to Savannah.

"You might wanna say a little prayer to St. Jude, too. He's the patron saint of hopeless cases." The old lady was on a ramble again. "You got a hope chest?"

"Huh?"

"I make hope chests fer all the men in my family 'cause men are basically hopeless. Do you want yer pillowcases monogrammed with M & S or S & M?"

Oh. My. God! "I might be hopeless, but I don't need any hope chest or pillow cases," he started to say.

But she had already hung up.

Despite his confusion, he was smiling.

Until he saw the look of fury on his mother's face.

"You're going to chase after that girl, aren't you?"

"I'm going to chase after both of my girls." He'd already tapped in numbers for information and asked for the airlines. While he waited, he turned to his mother. "How could you tell Savannah that I was dead?"

Her pale face got flushed. Then she attempted to defend her actions. "You might have been."

"That's pathetic."

"Matt, we're your family. We were only doing what we thought best for you."

He shook his head. "As far as I'm concerned, the only family I have is in Louisiana."

You could say it was a LeDeux invasion . . .

IN TWO MORE DAYS, Savannah and Katie would be leaving for Alaska.

Her car was up for sale on one of the Internet auto sites. The plane tickets were purchased. She had reservations at a bed and breakfast in Anchorage. She'd even put in applications for teaching at several schools, and the prospects looked good.

If she hadn't used up so much of her money making last minute purchases for their trip, she wouldn't be working these last days before departure. Savannah was owed two weeks' salary, which she doubted she would get if she weren't here on Friday, payday.

And she hadn't even had to sell her ring, which had been a real possibility there for a while. She'd pawned it twice a few years back, but then redeemed it, being the only thing Savannah had from Matt. She wanted to pass the ring on to his daughter one day.

"Jones, get your ass out here! You have three frickin' orders up."

Savannah grimaced as Hal Frankin's voice boomed at her through the door of the ladies' room. She could procrastinate only so long. She gave herself one last look-see in the mirror and cringed. A Daisy Mae blouse with a stretchy neckline, meant to be off the shoulders, was tucked into black shorts, very short shorts. On her feet were red high heels that already made her toes ache, and she hadn't even started her shift.

"I'm coming, I'm coming," she said as she ambled out.

Hal was leaning against the wall, arms folded over his bull-like chest, waiting for her. "What the hell is up with you?"

"I don't know what you mean."

"That outfit is supposed to show the tops of your boobs and half your butt cheeks. How'd you manage to make it look like librarian's day at a strip joint?"

A lot of tugging and seam loosening. "I'm wearing the damn thing."

"That's a good idea, actually."

"What?"

"You could do a strip routine as a prissy librarian with a nympho secret side."

Can I barf now? "I am not stripping. I've told you that a dozen times before."

"We'll see about that. Does CPS know you have a kid living in a car on the dangerous streets of the French Quarter?"

She gasped.

"Just kidding," he said, but she wasn't sure that he was. "You wanna keep this job?"

"Yes." *Hell, no!*

"Then stop bein' so—"

Just then, the chef yelled out, "Pick up 8, 9, 10. Mayday! The eggs are gettin' cold."

That was her cue. Thank God!

She rushed over to pick up her orders. As she was balancing a tray over her shoulder, she passed Celeste Arnaud coming off the stage. Celeste was stark naked, except for five-inch clear plastic heels and a garter filled with dollar bills. A cell phone was pressed to her ear.

"I told you, Sammy. You cannot eat Sweet Froots cereal for lunch. With that much sugar, you'll be bouncing off the walls. Tell Nana to make you a sandwich."

Hal was up on stage, revving up the crowd for the next dancer while Savannah served food to three tables. She took two more orders over to the counter, hot wing sausage and scrambled eggs, a Cluck Burger made with ground, boneless hot wings, and a Cobb salad with bits of hot wings substituting for bacon. Wincing at the shrill static of the sound system before it erupted with "Mustang Sally," she saw Sally Anderson, a college student who needed to supplement her scholarship money, come galloping out to loud cheers. She wore a cowboy hat, chaps, a G-string, boots, a garter, and a little vest that barely covered her breasts. There was much hooting and yelling and whistling, especially from the men sitting at the horseshoe-shaped bar that surrounded the stripper stage. And it wasn't even the noon rush yet.

In the old days when Savannah had to drive to work for her

teaching job in Georgia at seven a.m., she would be surprised to see cars already parked outside the X-rated stores along the highway. Therefore she wasn't all that surprised that men showed up twenty-four hours a day at Hal's to watch naked women while they ate. Hot wings and horndogs!

Savannah was wiping off tables when she noticed Tante Lulu. Honestly, she knew the interfering old busybody meant well, but she was asking way too many questions, some of which were downright painful to answer. Like, where was Katie's father and did Savannah love him and how come she wasn't with him now?

Finally, Savannah had exploded. "Because he's dead, dammit! No more questions."

That hadn't stopped the old lady, though. Instead, she'd urged her to come stay with her on Bayou Black, which had become a running thread in all their conversations.

"Why cain't you come stay at my cottage?"

Are you kidding? "Why would I want to do that?"

"A vacation? It's really nice down on the bayou, 'ceptin' fer the gator, but Useless . . . thass the gator's pet name . . . is harmless as long as you feed him Cheez Doodles."

My idea of a vacation is basking on the beach of some tropical island, not lolling around with an alligator that has a name. "I can't take a vacation. I need to work."

"Then, let Katie come and visit fer a spell."

Not in this lifetime! "Katie goes nowhere without me."

"I could give . . . uh, lend you some money."

And what strings would be attached? "No! Thanks, but no."

Frankly, Tante Lulu and what seemed to be a dozen family members who accompanied her on visits to the bar were the reason she had moved up the timeline for her departure. Their questions were getting too intrusive, and it made her uncomfortable that there were two lawyers, a police detective, and a newspaper reporter in the LeDeux family.

And now, Tante Lulu, her niece Charmaine, and some hunky guy in cowboy boots who was probably Charmaine's rancher husband sat down at an empty table, and the old lady beckoned her to come over. Savannah glanced over at Hal and raised five fingers to indicate she was taking her break.

Tante Lulu had on a Dorothy Hamill wig. It was a wedge cut and bright red. Matching polish covered her fake fingernails and toenails, which peeked out from a pair of high-heeled open-toed pumps, which were red, as well. She better be careful she doesn't trip on the uneven French Quarter sidewalks. The topper was the tight red spandex dress that showed off all her bony parts.

Charmaine was wearing the exact same dress, except hers was neon pink, which matched her lipstick and finger and toe nails, of course. Her long black hair was poufed up, Texas style. Where Tante Lulu looked a little ridiculous in the slut dress, Charmaine was one hot mama.

But wait. At an adjoining table was Tee-John, who was wearing a cop uniform, unbuttoned down to the waist. Beside him was what Savannah presumed was his wife, wearing the same spandex dress, hers in blue, squished over her very visible baby bump. Tee-John gave Savannah a little wave. His wife shrugged her shoulders, as if to say this wasn't her idea.

Remy, the pilot in the family, wore what else . . . an aviator jacket over a bare chest. His wife Rachel's spandex dress was jade green. Finally, there was René, an environmentalist/teacher/musician who wore a frottir or Cajun style washboard over his shoulders. He winked at her, which did not amuse his lawyer wife who wore black spandex and peered at Savannah over reading glasses perched on the end of her nose.

And there were other people as well. Probably friends or honorary family. All dressed with similar outrageousness.

Something strange is going on. Savannah turned on Tante Lulu. "Okay, I know it's not Halloween. So, what's the occasion?"

"Cain't a gal dress up if she wants to?"

In Crazy Hal's? Savannah arched her brows at Tante Lulu's attire. "Frederick's of the Bayou?"

"Nope. These dresses are family heirlooms, sort of. There's a dressmaker in Houma that can make one fer you."

"Uh."

Charmaine chuckled at Savannah's discomfort. She was probably subjected to the old lady's intrusiveness all the time. To give her credit, Charmaine treated her aunt with the utmost respect. All of her family did.

"You haven't met my husband yet, have you?" Charmaine glanced sideways, then gave a hard nudge to the cowboy stud, who was gaping at the stage where Sally was continuing her strip routine, now to "Pony" by Ginuwine. He almost fell off his chair before he righted himself. "This is Rusty, better known as the-husband-who-sleeps-on-the-couch-tonight. Rusty, this is the girl I was telling you about. Savannah Jones."

He nodded at Savannah.

Savannah wasn't about to be diverted. Turning back to Tante Lulu, she asked, "Why are you here again today?" She didn't care if she sounded rude. Her constant visits were annoying, even if she did mean well.

Tante Lulu patted her on the hand. "We was jist in the neighborhood."

Yeah, right. She noticed that the tables in front of them were being filled, and a lot of the customers were women. Here and there, folks were giving Tante Lulu a little wave. By now Hal should have been ordering her back to work, especially with the full house. But when she looked his way, he just smiled at her. She did a double take. Yep, the sleazeball was smiling at her.

Savannah rose to her feet, frowning with confusion. Her heart was racing as her body went on red alert. She had no idea what was going on, but she had a bad feeling that it involved her. "What have you done?" she asked Tante Lulu.

"Jist makin' a miracle, honey. A St. Jude kinda miracle."

Then, Tante Lulu and all of her family and friends put their heads, face down, on the tables. Until there was a drum roll on the stage where, miraculously, a band had appeared. The Swamp Rats. René, who was a member of the band, stepped up to the microphone. "We're not doing our Cajun Village People act today, despite our attire. Nope, we have somethin' else in mind." He held up a hand for silence. When you could have heard a pin drop, he crooned softly, "She's lost that lovin' feeling."

It was the line from that Righteous Brothers song, made famous by Tom Cruise and his buddy in the movie *Top Gun.* The band broke out into a raucous version of the song, and men and women who'd accompanied Tante Lulu stood, one by one, and sang the refrain as they snake-danced to the stage. Soon all of the LeDeux clan were up there, dancing and singing their little hearts out. Even the guys in the audience who should have been disappointed to have no nude women were clapping their enjoyment of this surprise entertainment.

Savannah realized that she was gaping and clicked her jaw shut. She was still confused, but not for long.

Tante Lulu stepped forward, and René adjusted the microphone to compensate for her height.

"We LeDeux allus like to step up ta help couples who have lost their way. With the aid of St. Jude and my good friend Hal, *thass* jist what were gonna do t'day."

"*Who* lost that lovin' fellin'?" Lucien LeDeux yelled at his aunt from the back of the stage.

"I thought you'd never ask." She raised a hand and pointed.

At Savannah.

The things a man will do for love . . .

MATT'S FIRST REACTION on entering Crazy Hal's was anger that Savannah had been forced to work in such a dive. Knowing the kind of person she was, he had no doubt that she'd been forced by her circumstances.

His second reaction was "Wow!" on seeing Savannah. Her golden blond hair hung in a straight swath down to her bare shoulders. She was wearing Daisy Duke shorts, an off-the-shoulder peasant blouse, and high heels. Holy frickin' wow!

He felt like an absolute dork wearing his dress blues on a hot New Orleans day. But according to the bayou matchmaker who'd orchestrated this whole scenario, the clothes were requisite for melting Savannah's heart. Tante Lulu had mentioned that something similar had worked for Remy, one of her nephews who had been a former Air Force pilot, except in that case the scenario involved a Village People routine. He figured his set-up was the lesser of two evils. At least he hoped so. He didn't trust that Cajun nutcase farther than he could throw her, which he'd been tempted to do on more than one occasion the past two days as she grilled him and prepped him to make sure he was worthy of Savannah.

Matt took more steps inside the club, still out of Savannah's range of vision. Savannah was talking to Tante Lulu, her niece Charmaine, and her husband, both of whom he'd met yesterday. Savannah did not look happy.

He would have preferred a private reunion with Savannah—*and please, God, let there be a reunion, let her be happy to see me*—but Tante Lulu wouldn't tell him where she was unless he agreed to her plan. Also involved were other members of her family, all of whom he'd met at one time or another out at Tante Lulu's bayou cottage.

When Tante Lulu had finally revealed her plan for him to reunite with Savannah, he'd protested. Vehemently. "I don't think I can do anything like that. Honestly, it's hard for me to do such things in public."

To which, she'd given him her version of the evil eye and said, "You gotta have faith, boy. Faith makes things possible, not easy."

Whatever the hell that meant!

Tee-John, the youngest of the nephews and a Fontaine police detective, had advised Matt to just go with the flow, that their aunt was like a bulldozer when she got an idea into her head. In fact, on the way here this morning, another nephew, Lucien, a lawyer, related, "My aunt is a well-known folk healer, but she's also noted for her matchmaking skills. In our family alone, she has finagled a surprise wedding, several Village People events, a cowboy kidnapping, and a pirate ball."

He had just stared at Luc with horror. In his ultra-conservative family, the most outrageous thing he'd ever seen was his mother's backyard picnic complete with china and crystal and silver.

Then he'd grinned. He liked the idea of a family that did outlandish things under the direction of the bayou dingbat. In fact, he liked the idea of such a family, period.

He was waiting now for a cue from said dingbat.

A woman in pigtails danced onto the stage, sucking on a lollipop and gyrating to Britney Spears' "Oops, I Did It Again." René went up to talk with some man; Matt wasn't certain about what and wasn't sure he wanted to know, especially since it included René slipping the man a few bills. Meanwhile, the now mostly nude Spears wannabe left the stage, dozens of dollar bills spilling out of her G-string.

She stopped in front of him and asked, "Are you going to strip?"

He was speechless.

"If so, I might stick around." She blinked her false eyelashes at him.

Matt found it rather hard to carry on a conversation with a stranger wearing only a G-string. "Lord, I hope not," he said.

She shrugged and walked off.

Then the Swamp Rats band went on stage. There was some talking by a band member. Then they played that song from Top Gun, which led to all the LeDeux clan getting up on stage. He knew because he'd seen them rehearse the routine in Tante Lulu's backyard.

By now, he was sweating bullets.

In the ensuing musical silence between sets, Tante Lulu peeked out of the side curtain on the stage and crooked her forefinger at him. With a deep inhale and exhale for courage (To Matt, this was harder than facing a band of Al-Qaeda.), he stepped forward.

Showtime!

Chapter Four

He wasn't a young Richard Gere. He was better . . .

SAVANNAH WAS mortified to be singled out so publicly. What was Tante Lulu thinking?

And about that "lost that lovin' feeling'" crap . . . did that mean the old lady was trying to fix her up with some guy? Like one of her extended LeDeux family. Well, she better not. Savannah was off to Alaska, and that was that!

Savannah ducked out of the spotlight when she heard the band start a new song: Joe Cocker's "Love Lifts Us Up Where We Belong." What an odd choice for strip music. She was just thinking that she hadn't heard it since she'd seen *An Officer and a Gentleman* years ago when, to her surprise, some military guy stepped onto the stage. A hunk in a spiffy blue military uniform. Even from this distance she could see the numerous bars and stars. A stripper? Since when did Hal hire male strippers? Hmmm. Maybe he was trying to attract more of a female clientele.

This day just kept getting stranger and stranger.

Oh, well. It was nothing to her. But why were all the LeDeuxs smiling and clapping?

She gave the guy another glance. He removed his dress hat, exposing a "high and tight" military haircut which didn't entirely tame the black curls that would rule if worn longer. Wearing a serious expression on his face, he jumped off the stage and headed in her direction, all the while ignoring the hoopla around him. She glanced over her shoulder to see if someone was standing behind her. Nope.

She blinked. Then blinked again.

Slowly, she began to recognize him, and his similarity to her daughter, right down to the beautiful caramel-brown eyes.

"Matt?" she choked out. This was impossible. He was dead. Wasn't he?

If he isn't dead, where the hell has he been all these years?

Immediately, she tamped her temper down and rejoiced that he was still alive. Katie's daddy was still alive!

Oh, no! Has he come to take Katie from me?

He didn't give her a chance to ask any questions, or turn tail and run. Tossing his hat to the side, he lifted her by the waist so her feet dangled off the floor, and hugged her so tight she could barely breathe. "Oh, God, Savannah, I have missed you so much," he whispered against her neck.

She pulled back to look at him and smacked him on the chest. "I thought you were dead." She would have given him an earful, but he was kissing her like there was no tomorrow. And then she was kissing him back.

In between kisses, she said, "You never wrote to me."

And he replied, "I never got your letters."

"Your mother is a witch."

"Tell me something I don't already know."

"I'll never forgive you for leaving me all these years."

"I'll never forgive myself."

"Where have you been?"

"POW."

"Oh, Matt!" she cried.

"Why aren't you teaching?"

"Lost my job. Going to Alaska."

"Not anymore."

"Your mother told me—"

"I know. Forget about her."

"Were you hurt?"

"I'm okay now."

"How did you find me?"

"I was searching for a long time, but it was Tante Lulu who found me."

Tante Lulu! I should have known.

"I love you, Savannah. I never stopped. Do you still love me?"

How could he even ask that question? "Forever."

Everyone in the restaurant was standing and cheering now, even Hal.

"We need to talk in private, sweetheart," Matt said, setting her down.

She didn't care who saw them. She kept touching Matt's face and shoulders, as if to convince herself that he was really here.

"Mommy!"

Tante Lulu was holding Katie's hand and walking toward them.

Matt gasped and murmured before dropping to one knee to put himself on Katie's level, "She's beautiful."

So, he already knew. Tante Lulu again, she concluded, but she couldn't be angry. Instead, she smiled. She could see the love in Matt's eyes already.

Tante Lulu, dabbing her eyes with a St. Jude handkerchief, leaned down and whispered something in Katie's ear. Her eyes went wide, then she launched herself at Matt. "Daaa-ddyyy!" With her little legs wrapped around his waist and her arms locked in a death grip around his neck, Matt stood and looked Savannah's way, mouthing, "Thank you."

Tante Lulu came up beside Savannah and squeezed her hand. "Mission accomplished."

"I owe you so much." Savannah's voice was raspy with emotion.

"Jist thank St. Jude. He's the go-to guy."

It's true. Men do have only one thing on their minds. Women do, too . . .

REUNIONS WERE sweet, and Matt loved getting to know his daughter, all thanks to one interfering Cajun busybody. And Tante Lulu sure knew how to throw a good party, what she called a *fais do do*, at her cottage down on the bayou.

As thankful as he was, gratefulness went only so far. For three hours Matt had been repeating "Pleased to meet you's,"

"Yes, that's a Silver Star," "No, I couldn't eat another bite of Peachy Praline Cobbler Cake," "Another cold beer would be nice," "Yeah, Afghanistan is a royal SNAFU for the military," "My plans are up in the air right now, but I'm a jarhead at heart." Now, he was dying to get out of this monkey suit, and he was more than ready for something else. In fact, he was desperate for something else.

Savannah.

Alone.

Preferably naked.

He didn't want to be rude, especially after all Tante Lulu had done for him, but enough was enough.

"Let's get out of here," he whispered in Savannah's ear as he came up behind her. She was standing in front of the St. Jude birdbath talking to Charmaine. Cajun zydeco music provided a lively backdrop to the colorful bayou setting, complete with slow-moving stream, ancient trees with hanging moss, and the overpowering scent of tropical-like flowers.

Tante Lulu had already offered to keep Katie for the night; so, they were all right in that regard. And Katie was ecstatic at the prospect of spending more time with Tee-John's son Etienne, Charmaine's daughter, and all her new found LeDeux friends. Right now, they were tossing Cheez Doodles to an alligator, *of all things*, named Useless, *of all things*, under the supervision of Remy, whose pet the beast had originally been. Tante Lulu had also given Matt the keys to her car to use temporarily since his own vehicle was back at Fort Dix.

Savannah turned and wrapped her arms loosely around his shoulders, her usually dark blue eyes lightened with emotion, the way he remembered them being when they . . . well, he couldn't think about that now without embarrassing himself. She'd changed from her restaurant "uniform" into a blue and white checked sun dress with thin straps in deference to the heat. Her pretty blond hair was tucked behind her ears, also in deference to the heat. He was pleased to see that she'd taken his engagement ring off the chain around her neck and put it back on her finger, where it belonged. It about killed him that she'd had to pawn it a couple times just to eat.

"What'd you have in mind?" Savannah asked in a sultry voice she seemed to have cultivated in his absence. He couldn't wait to see what else she'd cultivated.

"I want to make love to you, honey. Every which way I can, and then some," he told her, and he didn't care if Charmaine heard him, either. "I have a lot of years to make up for. So, what do you say? Want me to rock your world?"

"That depends. Can I rock your world, too?" she replied saucily, reaching up to kiss, then nip, at his chin.

To hell with chins! He wanted kisses in other places, lots of other places. He pinched her butt and said, "We'll rock the night away, both of us. Guar-an-teed, as the Cajuns say."

"Holy Sac-au-lait! I'm gettin' turned on just listenin' to you two," Charmaine said, with a laugh. Then, she yelled, "Rusty! Let's go home!"

Matt smiled and tucked Savannah into his side with an arm over her shoulders. "I hope you brought that Daisy Duke outfit with you. I have plans." He waggled his eyebrows at her.

"Hey, I have one of those outfits at home, believe it or not," Charmaine told them.

As if I care! And, yeah, he would believe it or her. Charmaine was the first to call herself "a bimbo with class."

When Rusty answered his wife's call and stepped up beside her, she smiled at him. "Guess what, sweetie? When we get home, we're gonna play a game."

Rusty's groan indicated he wasn't too excited about the suggestion.

"Lil' Abner and Daisy Mae."

Now Rusty was excited. He smiled, a lazy twitch of the lips, and winked at his wife.

Savannah sighed. Now, *she* was excited.

Charmaine slanted her eyes with a sideways glance at her husband and licked her Screw-Me Red, probably Botoxed lips, real slow.

"Darlin'," Rusty drawled out. "I am so good at games."

Matt was getting turned on watching them all. Time to get

this show on the road. Grabbing Savannah's hand, he led her over to Tante Lulu, who was at the folding table still piled high with food, everything from shrimp étouffée to crawfish and shrimp gumbo to lazy bread to sweet pralines. Pitchers of sweet tea, beer, and soft drinks on ice.

"We're going to leave now," Savannah said, giving the old lady a hug. "Thank you so much for keeping Katie overnight. We'll be back in the morning to pick her up."

"My pleasure, sweetie. When you get here, we'll start makin' plans fer the weddin'."

We, Matt thought. *Uh-oh.*

"You've done enough," Savannah was quick to say as she squeezed his hand, sharing his dismay. "We'll probably just elope or have a courthouse wedding." She glanced at him. "We really haven't discussed details yet."

In fact, they'd had almost no time alone at all since he'd arrived at the strip club. Dammit!

"You cain't do that!" Tante Lulu declared. "You gotta have a priest, or a preacher if yer not Catholic, ta seal the deal, proper like. Doesn't hafta be a big weddin'. Mebbe jist yer family and friends, Savannah. Matt's family and friends. And all us LeDeuxs. The reception hall at our Lady of the Bayou Church kin handle up ta two hundred people, in a squeeze."

Matt stiffened at the idea of his parents at his wedding. "I don't have any family to speak of, and my friends are mostly military, scattered around the world."

"Two hundred people!" Savannah squeaked out. "I don't have any family, and I don't have any close friends."

Matt's anger rose once again, knowing she'd been forced to avoid friendships because of his parents' threats. Hard to have a girlfriend, or guy friend, over for a drink when you're living in a car. He blew out a frustrated exhale and said, "I wouldn't invite my parents to a dog fight, let alone my wedding."

"Now, now," Tante Lulu said, "they're still yer family. Remember, it was St. Jude who brought you two t'gether, and he's all 'bout forgiveness."

"Not gonna happen," Matt insisted.

"Don'tcha be worryin' none. I'm plannin' on havin' a little sit-down with yer mother on Sunday after Mass. A come-ta-Jesus talk, ya might say."

Oh, shit!

"I invited her ta lunch at Big Butch's Crab Shanty."

Oh, shit!

"I'd like to be a fly on the wall at that meeting," Savannah whispered to him, a mischievous grin teasing at her lips. "If anyone can straighten a person out, Tante Lulu can."

Or drive them bat shit crazy. "Go for it!" he conceded, "but I'll tell you up front, I won't let them ruin a happy day. My dad's not so bad, but my mother could make a scene."

"Listen, boy, some folks have their minds mixed up and permanently set, like concrete. What we gotta do is chisel away."

Good luck with that. My mother is chisel-proof. Matt rolled his eyes. "She would stand out like a sore thumb among all you good folks."

Tante Lulu nodded. "Like pickles in a praline."

"Good example," Matt said. He'd love to see his mother's face if Tante Lulu made that comparison to her face.

"I know how ta turn a pickle inta a pecan. Leave it all ta me."

And they did, which was probably a big mistake, but Matt had other things on his mind.

"One more thing," Tante Lulu said.

He couldn't suppress his groan. Savannah choked back a laugh.

"Here." Tante Lulu handed him a key.

He frowned with confusion. "You already gave me the car key."

"This is another key." Tante Lulu waggled her penciled-in eyebrows at him. "I got you two a room at the Hubba Hubba Ding Ding Motel. I coulda reserved you a room at the Marriott or Comfort Suites in Houma, but the Hubba is closer, only 'bout ten minutes away."

Matt liked the idea of closer. A lot.

"Plus, they got vibrating beds at the Hubba, I hear. You

know, the kind ya put in a quarter and it shakes ya up like a milkshake."

No, Matt didn't know, but he was game for anything if it involved him and Savannah, horizontal, naked, etc.

He grinned.

Savannah blushed.

Tee-John stepped up then and looped an arm over Tante Lulu's little shoulders. "Auntie! You never rented *me* any motel rooms."

"*Thass* 'cause you was boinkin' every girl up and down the bayou."

"Boinkin'?" Tee-John laughed and put a hand over his heart. "I am wounded."

"Yer *gonna* be wounded if Celine gets her hands on you. Where is she anyways?"

"In the house. Peeing. For about the tenth time since we got here. Plus, she's feeling nauseous."

"I got herbs fer that. Do you think she'd take ground-up gator testicles mixed with frog spit and a little Pepto fer color?"

"Ab-so-lute-ly!" Tee-John said with a straight face. "But let's not tell her the ingredients . . . until later."

On that note, Matt and Savannah escaped . . . uh, left the party. Matt couldn't stop kissing Savannah as they walked around the side of the cottage leading to the detached one-car garage. He pressed her up against the side of the cottage and kissed her until his knees about gave way, and he had really strong knees. She kissed him while he attempted to raise the old fold-up wooden door on the garage, and he almost dropped the blasted thing on her toes.

They stopped kissing then as they gaped at their transport. A huge tank of a car, so big it almost touched the sides of the garage. It was a 1960s era lavender Chevy Impala convertible. There was a St. Jude wobble head on the dashboard and a bumper sticker that read, "Not so close. I'm not that kind of girl."

"We should have known better when she told us her car had a name . . . Lillian," Savannah said.

"You named your car Betty," he pointed out.

"That's different."

It took some maneuvering to get the vehicle out of the garage, but once on the way, they soon discovered one of the advantages of these old cars. Bench seats. The engineers who invented bucket seats hadn't taken into account the benefits to a guy of one-arm driving with his honey sitting close. Real close. He would bet his back pay that Tante Lulu knew the value of those bed-like seats from experience back in the day. And maybe even later in her outrageous life. The old bird had game.

He was cruising down the one-lane road, driving with his left hand, his right arm around Savannah's shoulders, hip to hip, Frank Sinatra crooning on the eight-track tape deck. With the rag top up, they were cocooned in their own private world, unseeing in the dusky light of early evening of the quaint countryside era passing by, redolent of another era. Crab shacks and one-pump gas stations. Neat cottages of pastel stucco. Homemade signs advertising, "Fresh Eggs. Sweet Butter. Okra." An occasional derelict auto or kitchen sink sitting in someone's front yard. A sofa on the front porch.

When Savannah put a hand on his thigh, he almost ran off the road. He hadn't engaged in foreplay in a car since he was a teenager.

When his right hand happened to meander downward and touch her breast, she moaned. A sweet, poignant sound that acted as the most potent aphrodisiac. Not that his libido needed any jumpstart.

When Savannah raised her head and kissed his neck, pleasure rippled over all the fine hairs of his body like a warm breeze on cool grass.

When he kissed the top of her head and said in a voice husky with emotion, "I love you, Savannah. You are what kept me going in the hard days of captivity."

"Oh, Matt!" He felt her tears against his neck and hugged her tighter. "I never stopped loving you, even when I thought you were . . . gone." He could tell she didn't want to say the word *dead.*

"No sad times tonight," he ordered with a mock growl.

By the time they arrived at the garish Hubba Hubba Ding Ding Motel five minutes later, Matt was thankful that, key in hand, they didn't have to face any people at a registration desk. Not just because he and Savannah were loopy with lust for each other, but because he doubted he could have put two coherent words together, not even, "Room! Now!"

He had trouble unlocking the door with his shaking hands, but it finally opened, and he was vaguely aware of a dim light coming from a bedside lamp. They stumbled into the room, slamming the door behind them. Quicker than he could say "G.I. Joe With a Hard-on," he had her backed up against the wall. At the same time, he was kissing her voraciously, even as he removed his jacket and stepped out of his shoes. Thank God for multi-tasking!

She was no better, undoing his shirt so fast buttons were flying.

He undid the back zipper on her dress.

She undid the zipper on his pants.

For a moment, Matt saw an explosion of stars behind his closed eyelids. G.I. Joe was going to end this game before it began if he didn't get his act together. He inhaled sharply, then exhaled.

When he opened his eyes, Savannah was staring at him with sex-hazy eyes. Her lips were parted, and she was breathing as heavily as he was. Even better, he saw that Savannah's dress had fallen to her waist with the straps hanging from her arms. She was wearing no bra, and her breasts were perfect twin globes the size of half oranges. The nipples were erect against the backdrop of rose-hued aureoles.

"So pretty!" he murmured, and couldn't resist leaning down to lick one nipple, then the other.

Savannah released a long keening wail of carnal pleasure. "Ooooooh!"

That's it! I can't wait any longer. He picked her up by the waist, turned, and almost tripped over his unzipped trousers that were bagging about his knees. Tossing Savannah onto the bed, he crawled up over her. Instinctively, even as he was back to kissing her, deep kissing, a wet exchange of tongues and teeth and hungry lips, he raised the hem of her dress and tore off her silk panties. Also, instinctively, he assumed since Savannah wasn't usually so bold, she reached into his briefs and took his rampant erection in hand.

I didn't intend to do it. Honest, honey, I didn't! But before he knew what was happening he was deep inside her hot, moist body where the inner muscles were clutching him in welcome, like a soldier just home from the wars. Which he was. But this was not the way for reunion sex to go. It should be a leisurely, exploring, re-acquaintance of familiar and yet strange bodies. A slow build-up of arousal. Lots of whispered avowals of love and promises of a future together.

Maybe I could do a bit of backtracking here. He raised his head, arms braced on his elbows, about to apologize for his clumsy haste.

Instead of looking disappointed, or even angry, she smiled up at him and said, "Welcome home, soldier."

Forget backtracking! It would appear that G.I. Joe just got hot damn lucky. "Oh, baby!" Looking at her beautiful blue eyes, he recalled the precious sapphire pendant he'd purchased after his deployment but before being taken prisoner by those evil Taliban rebels. He'd seen it in a jeweler's window and was reminded of her. "By the way, honey, wait until you see what I got for you!"

"In your rucksack?" she teased, wriggling her hips from side to side for emphasis.

He pinched her butt. "Not that. Back in my apartment at Fort Dix. Something I bought for you when I first arrived overseas almost six years ago."

"And you kept it, even thinking that I'd left you?"

"Like you, I couldn't stop the loving and maybe even, unconsciously, the hoping."

She put a hand up to his face. "Oh, sweetheart. I don't need presents. All I need is you."

"Ditto," he said and kissed her softly. Then not so softly.

"I'm sorry, but I can't wait. I need you, baby. I'll do better next time, I prom—"

"I can't wait either," she admitted shyly. Then, not so shyly, she arched her hips off the bed and wrapped her legs around his waist.

Wait! Wait a damn minute! "Oh, crap! I forgot a condom," he gasped out. "A good soldier never forgets a condom. Where did I put them? How could I—"

"If you stop now, I might have to kill you, good soldier or not." She glanced to the left. "I thought I saw . . . yes!" There was a condom sitting on the bedside table, compliments of the Hubba.

That was all the encouragement he needed. He withdrew, rolled on the condom one-handed, and plunged back into her clasping folds, long and slow. But only twice. Then his strokes became short and hard, and her clasping was a constant erotic signal that she was enjoying him as much as he was enjoying her. The friction of his erection against her folds was beyond bliss, erotic torture of the best kind.

Anything else that happened was by pure reflex. His hands caressing her everywhere. His lips kissing everywhere. Murmuring his appreciation of her various body parts, some of the words more graphic that he would use if he were in his right mind. Not that he was in his wrong mind. No mind, that's how to describe him.

She was caressing and kissing and murmuring, too. "Don't ever leave me again," she pleaded.

"Never!" he promised.

Her body stiffened, and he sensed her approaching orgasm, not that she'd hadn't already climaxed, but they were minis compared to what was coming up. He braced himself, holding off his own completion until she screamed and began to convulse rapidly around him. Only then did he throw his head back and roar out his own climax. There might have been violins playing with a whole orchestra backup, or maybe he was just high on supreme male satisfaction.

For several long moments, he lay heavily over her. When

his rapid breathing slowed to a mere pant, he raised himself and said, "I love you, Savannah."

She was fast asleep.

He remembered that about her then . . . how, when she'd had a particularly powerful orgasm, her body shut down into sleep mode. With utter male pride, he grinned. G.I. Joe had not lost his game! A guy liked knowing he could affect his woman so strongly. And vice versa, of course.

Easing himself carefully out of her, he slid off the bed. His shirt had been unbuttoned and hung half off his shoulders. His pants were puddled at his feet. And Savannah was even worse. She wore only one high-heeled sandal; the other was over by the door. Her dress was shoved down to her waist, one strap broken, and the hem hiked up. Her legs were splayed open, exposing blond curls glistening from their sex. A scrap of fabric lay on the floor, what remained of her panties. *Penthouse Forum* couldn't have painted a better picture of a male fantasy.

He went into the bathroom and washed himself off. Then he came back into the bedroom, getting his first real look at their surroundings. "Oh, my God!"

The room was red. Everywhere. The walls, the carpet, the lamp shade, the bed spread, even the hanging chandelier—yes, there was a small crystal chandelier over the king size bed—had red bulbs. And cupids . . . there were cupids everywhere: carved into the headboard, the base of the lamp, the dresser pulls, pictures on the walls. Holy hell! He peered closer at one painting. Did cupids really do *that*?

Tante Lulu had been right. There was a small coin box at the end of the bed that read, "Good Vibrations, high, medium, low, four quarters for five minutes." He sure hoped he had enough change in his pants. If not, he was running to the nearest convenience store. Thankfully, he had a few coins. He put four quarters in, but nothing happened. Oh, well!

Matt glanced at his wristwatch. Only nine p.m. At least ten hours until they had to pick up Katie. With a grin, he grabbed something from his wallet, then lay himself down on his side next to Savannah on the bed. He tickled her nose, making it twitch, until she finally opened her eyes.

She woke immediately. Smiling up at him, she said, "Hi!" There was a world of meaning in that greeting.

"Have I told you lately that I love you?" she asked.

"Not nearly enough," he said, trailing a fingertip from her chin to her breastbone, which called her attention to her carnal disarray. He loved the full-body flush that swept over her then.

"I have something for you," he said as he helped her remove her clothing.

"You already told me. Something back in your Fort Dix apartment."

"No. This is a different something." He whipped out an accordion strip of foil goodies. At least twelve condoms.

She laughed. "A bit overconfident, aren't you?"

"Sweetheart, you have no idea," he said.

Just then, the bed vibrations kicked in, and an old Beach Boys song blasted out from a radio next to the TV.

"Good Vibrations," for sure. He laughed as he rolled over and on top of her, spreading her legs with his knees. Then she laughed and rolled so that she was on the top, her knees straddling his belly.

Then, they both stopped laughing.

The vibrations that ensued came only partly from the mattress.

Epilogue

Tante Lulu always gets her own way . . .

TANTE LULU PREENED with satisfaction as Captain Matthew Carrington and Savannah Jones were married in a small Houma chapel with a reception to follow at Our Lady of the Bayou Church reception hall. Everyone came around to her way of thinking, eventually.

Tante Lulu gave the bride away. She was dressed to the nines for the occasion in a peach chiffon cocktail dress and matching pumps that pinched her toes from the get-go. No matter! Her peach-dyed orthopedic shoes were stowed in the car for later dancing. Today she wore her own gray curls with an orange headband studded with rhinestones. She'd had her make-up and nails done at Charmaine's salon. Coral Satin was her color of the day.

Matthew and his best friend, Lt. James Singleton, who'd flown in especially from Kuwait, both wore dress blues. More than a few women sighed.

"There's something about a man in uniform," Charmaine was heard to remark, then quickly add, "Cowboys, too," when her husband gave her a wounded scowl.

"A military uniform on a man is what we usta call widow bait duds," Tante Lulu recalled, overhearing Charmaine.

"Any uniform, really. Give me a fireman any day," Charmaine agreed, fanning her face with a program. "Oops. Just kidding, Rusty."

"Hey, *chère*, how about a police uniform?" Tee-John added as he passed by. "Whenever I want a quickie, I just have to arrive home in uniform over lunch hour."

Celine, looking pretty as a waddling hippo in a blue

maternity dress, elbowed her husband. "Idiot! You don't wear a uniform anymore."

"I could," he insisted with a wink.

Tante Lulu had wanted an archway of swords leading from the chapel, but Matthew rejected that idea. "You can't have a one-soldier archway."

"Some of us LeDeux could hold swords."

Matthew and Savannah had both said, "No!"

The bride wore a pearl-white suit with matching high heels. Around her neck hung a precious blue sapphire in a platinum setting, the groom's gift, which had been purchased somewhere overseas long ago. Also a complement to her eye color was the bouquet of blue irises and white roses that Matthew had given her. Her hair was upswept under a small pillbox hat with a demi-veil.

Matthew whispered to her as they stood at the altar, "I hope we have children someday with blue eyes like yours."

"Not right away, though," she whispered back, "and I prefer golden brown eyes, like yours."

"Hah! It might be sooner than you both think," Tante Lulu joined in the conversation, except her whisper was loud enough to be heard in the front row where Matthew's mother and father sat. His mother looked as if she'd swallowed a lemon.

The minister, about to begin the ceremony, shushed them all, with a special wagging of the finger at Tante Lulu. They were old friends.

A baby? Sooner than they thought? Matthew and Savannah looked at each other in question. Did Tante Lulu know something they didn't? After all, she did have an unusual connection with a saint, didn't she?

Charmaine acted as matron of honor. She wore a suit, too, but hers was lavender and lots tighter. She would have preferred red, but Tante Lulu warned her not to outshine the bride.

The flower girl was Katherine Carrington, of course. The five-year-old, in a frothy confection of pink and white ruffles, flashed a toothless grin during the entire wedding. Having a daddy was like getting a birthday and Christmas gift all wrapped in one package, Katie was heard telling Etienne.

To which, Etienne replied, "I'd rather get a video game."

Overhearing him, Tante Lulu swatted the little boy on his rump, chastising, "Don'tcha ever talk like that, or you'll be sittin' in the corner for an hour, jist like yer daddy usta do."

Once the traditional and rather demure wedding was over, they headed over to the reception hall where René's band, The Swamp Rats, was already setting up.

Matthew's mother, once resigned to the wedding and informed that she was welcome only if she behaved, had wanted them to be married in an area country club that had a formal garden for weddings. She even offered to pay. Needless to say, she was not happy with the little chapel, but she managed to survive. Harder for her to accept was the reception, not just that it was being held in a church hall, but the Cajun tone to the whole affair. When they arrived in the church parking lot, Mrs. Carrington almost had a heart attack. They were greeted from the open doors of the hall by a loud and rowdy version of "Louisiana Saturday Night." Some of the invited guests even yelled out, "Yee-haw," and others, that age-old Rebel call.

With a hand to her heart, Mrs. Carrington addressed Tante Lulu, "But we're not Cajun."

"Honey . . ." Tante Lulu began.

That alone caused Mrs. Carrington to bristle.

". . . there are three ways a person kin become a Cajun. By birth. By marriage. And by the back door. Yer son and Savannah are now honorary Cajuns. They came in by my back door."

"Grandpa! Grandma!" Katie came racing toward the couple, whom she'd been introduced to for the first time this morning.

Mr. Carrington hunkered down to Katie's level, uncaring of the wrinkles in his thousand dollar suit, and gave her a big hug. Mrs. Carrington, whose designer dress probably cost more than most cars in the parking lot, didn't scrooch down, but the smile that melted the constant frown on her face was a good sign. Maybe she wasn't so bad, after all.

Later, Tante Lulu brought a late arrival over and introduced him to Matthew and Savannah. "Matthew, this is Major General Paul Duvall from Fort Polk, here in Loo-zee-anna. Paul, this is Captain Matthew Carrington. He's a war hero."

Matthew cringed at the introduction and cringed even more when he realized the old lady's motive.

"Wouldn't it be nice if Matthew could be assigned to Fort Polk soz he and his family kin live right here on the bayou?"

Savannah was the one to cringe then. It was one thing for Tante Lulu to interfere in their personal lives, but quite another for her to mess with Matthew's professional career.

The major put up a hand to halt their coming protests and laughed. "Now, Tante Lulu, that's something to be decided by me and Captain Carrington and a lot of high-ups."

"I know higher-ups," Tante Lulu said, a little miffed at their lack of appreciation for her efforts.

"I'm sure you do," they all said as one.

"For now, I'll be returning to Fort Dix with Savannah and Katie. We'll see what happens from there," Matthew told Tante Lulu in a conciliatory tone.

After all the dancing and eating and drinking and toasts, Matthew and Savannah were about to begin their last dance, a Cajun version of Garth Brooks' "The Dance" being played by the band. Soon they would be off to a short honeymoon in the Bahamas. They were taking their daughter with them.

As they moved slowly together in the dance, unaware of others joining them on the dance floor, Savannah said with tears misting her eyes, "I'm so happy. I don't know what the future holds, but this is such a great start."

"I know what the future holds," Matthew declared, swiping one of her tears with his thumb. "It will be whatever we make it and a lot of that Cajun philosophy that Tante Lulu keeps spouting."

Savannah smiled. "*Laissez le bons temp rouler?* Let the good times roll?"

"Guar-an-teed!" Matt answered in an exaggerated Cajun accent.

Tante Lulu danced by in a lively two-step with the elderly

butcher Gustave Boudreaux. She raised her eyes upward and whispered, “Thanks again, St. Jude. Another match made in heaven!”

The End

Tante Lulu's Beignets

History: Beignets (pronounced BEN-yea) have long been a Southern Louisiana specialty, particularly in New Orleans where they were made most famous by the French Quarter's Café du Monde. Best served with café au lait, especially for breakfast, beignets are considered the forerunner of modern doughnuts, minus the holes. Nothing more than fried pieces of raised dough sprinkled profusely with powdered sugar, the beignet has to be tasted to be appreciated. Tante Lulu loves to serve them to her guests.

Ingredients:

1 envelope dry yeast

1/2 c. warm water

4-5 c. flour

1 c. evaporated milk

1/2 c. granulated sugar

1/2 c. shortening (or ½ c. canola oil, or 3 tsp. softened butter)

1 X-large egg, or 2 small eggs, beaten

1 tsp. salt

2 c. powdered sugar

Oil for deep frying

Directions:

Mix water, granulated sugar, and yeast in a bowl and set aside for a half hour. Beat together the egg/s, salt, and evaporated milk and add to the yeast mixture. Stir in half of the flour, then add the shortening. The remaining flour should be added a little at a time until you have the right consistency . . . a soft dough that is not sticky. Do not knead. Place the dough in a greased bowl (or one sprayed with non-stick oil), cover, and refrigerate overnight.

Next day, punch the dough down and roll on a floured surface to 1/4 to 1/2 inch thickness. Cut into two-inch squares (bigger or smaller, depending on preference).

Preheat oil to roughly 375 degrees or until a drop of water sizzles in the pan. Lower the squares into the hot oil and brown on both sides. Drain on brown paper (a grocery bag will do) or paper towels. Roll the warm beignets in a generous amount of powdered sugar, or shake them in a bag of powdered sugar. Yum!

[A shortcut: My mother, who was by no means a Southerner and was in fact of Polish descent, used to make something similar that is called chrusciki. But she used frozen bread dough. After it had risen, she dropped finger pinchfuls of the dough into the hot oil. In her case, she rolled the final product in granulated sugar. These were not nearly as light or delicious as true beignets, but for today's working mother (and my mother was just that), it did in a pinch.]

About the Author: Sandra Hill

Sandra Hill is the bestselling author of more than thirty romantic humor novels. Whether they be historicals, contemporaries, time travels, or Christmas novellas, whether they be Vikings, Cajuns, Navy SEALs or sexy Santas, the common element in all her books is humor.

As the mother of four sons and the loooong-time wife of a stock broker, Sandra says that she had to develop a sense of humor as a survival skill in the all-male bastion she calls home. (Even her German shepherd is a male.) And as a newspaper journalist, before turning to fiction, she managed to find a lighter side to even the darkest stories.

It's been said that love makes the world go 'round, but in Sandra's world, love with a dash of laughter, makes it spin.

Made in the USA
San Bernardino, CA
01 July 2014